AFTER THE ANGEL MILL

AFTER THE ANGEL MILL

CAROL BRUNEAU

*For Patti,
with best wishes.*

Carol Bruneau

CORMORANT BOOKS

Published with the assistance of the Canada Council, the Ontario Arts Council, the Department of Heritage, and the Government of Ontario through the Ministry of Culture, Tourism and Recreation.

'The Accident' has been published in *New Maritimes*; 'Keeping House' will appear in *The Fiddlehead* and 'Homefires' in *A Room of One's Own*.

The poem on page 38 is from the personal collection of John O'Donnell at St. Francis Xavier University in Antigonish, and has previously appeared in the *Sydney Daily Post*. The author could not be traced.

Edited by Gena K. Gorrell.

Author photo by Julian Beveridge.

Cover from a watercolour and pastel, *In Cranberry Once . . .* (19" x 24", 1982) by Ellison Robertson.

Cover design by Thom Pritchard at Artcetera Graphics.

Printed and bound in Canada.

Published by Cormorant Books Inc.
RR 1, Dunvegan, Ontario K0C 1J0

Canadian Cataloguing in Publication Data

Bruneau, Carol, 1956-
    After the angel mill : short stories

ISBN 0-920953-91-3

    I. Title.

PS8553.R854A75 1995   C843'.54   C95-900647-8
PR9199.3.B78A65 1995

In memory of my mother, Marion

Table of Contents

Milk

In memory of Myrtle Davis, pregnant with her tenth child when her husband, William, was killed by company police during the 1925 coal miners' strike in Cape Breton. Davis was shot coming home from a neighbour's with a baby bottle of milk.

January 1926. Music and flowers, those were the things I loved most. The things that led me to Thomas Gillis too, I suppose. Delphiniums like you wouldn't believe at his family's home— a blue like the ocean and the sky mixed together, like bright ink swirled in a glass of water. I used to think his eyes were the same colour when we started courting.

But it was music got us together in the first place. I don't know if I should be happy about that or sad, sad that the beauty of things gets lost somehow, worn like polish off the floor. We met at a dance, you see. I remember it so well even now, waiting for the doctor to come, the sounds of old sheets being ripped and water boiling downstairs.

I'm calm this time, I've been through it before. Mama says it gets faster with your second, and the next one, and the next, till they almost slide out of you like your body's made of rubber. So I'll lie here on my side, breathing in and out real slow like she says, and try to put myself somewhere far, far away. Sprout wings and take flight, until the pains get too bad and bring me back to earth.

*

June 1924. My sister Mary Beth was there, and my brother Dan. It was the first dance of the summer in the little hall out by the point. I was twenty, Mary Beth and Dan a few years older. It was all the rage to go to a dance in the country, and the three of us got a ride out there in a wagon with some fellas Dan knew. Only a couple of years ago, though it seems like another lifetime now.

I still have the dress I wore, cream-colour with fine brown polka-dots, hanging amongst the aprons and workdresses in my closet. And the hat, a loose-brimmed brown velvet with a lovely cream rose. This was before the company shut down its store—Papa brought it home, though I hate to think what it cost. Usually such a thing was frowned on, but Papa thought it matched my hair, thick and dark brown, braided around my head. He said I could have it if I promised not to get my hair bobbed like the other girls. So I let him buy it for me, though I knew it would set him back. We were always trying so hard to keep ahead of our tally at the pluck-me store, have Papa bring home his pay without half of it taken off.

It was just getting dark, the sun a red slit in the sky over the black spruces, music drifting out of the hall to the road. My hat nearly flew under the wheels into the mud as I was climbing out of the wagon, it being breezy by the water. One of the fellas in the wagon took my hand to help me down, but I pulled it away just in time to save my hat. Good thing, I suppose, as it was the hat that drew Thomas. Or so he used to say, before we got married.

The dance had started; the fiddler was already in a lather on stage, both knees flying up from his kitchen chair, the woman at the piano wiping her forehead with a little hanky in between tunes. The hall was packed from the door to the stage, couples promenading, swirling and stepping up and down, their tapping feet like thunder on the shiny wooden floor. Along the benches on one side were some men, smoking and laughing amongst themselves, not paying much attention to the bench of women opposite. A couple of Mama's friends were there, all dolled up in fancy black shoes and Sunday dresses, their hair in neat spit-curls. And some girls I knew from town, most of them with fellas.

I noticed Thomas right off, standing outside the door. Who wouldn't've, him with that black-black hair and eyes that almost matched its blue sheen? Eyes like drift ice on a fine April day. Caught me looking at him, he did, before I could look away. He lit a cigarette and half smiled, half nodded—shyly, I thought. Respectfully. I followed my brother and sister inside and Mary Beth and I found a spot on the bench. We sat there watching the dancers twirling and marching in square sets, elbows sawing the air to the shrill scrape and moan of the bow. It was hot and smoky in spite of the breeze billowing out the curtains from the pitch-black windows, and I worried about staining my dress under the arms.

After a while Thomas sauntered in and found a spot right across from me. I tried not to look at him, concentrating instead on the dancers' feet, the frantic beat of their soles on the hardwood. The steps were none I recognized so I was just as glad nobody was asking me to dance.

Then the woman on stage left to get a drink of water and the fiddler started playing "Skye Boat Song", slow and mournful, drawing his bow back and forth slowly and deliberately as a butcher slicing meat. The dancers thinned out a little, most of them flopping down out of breath, laughing and chattering. You could just catch the deep notes, a sad low drawl that sent shivers up my spine. I closed my eyes and listened, listened till all there was in the hall was that fiddler jump-cutting the strings with his bow. The touch of cool fingers on my wrist nearly sent me out of my skin.

"Dance?" he said, staring at me. He was small and slender-boned, not quite a head taller than me, and he spoke in a quiet deep voice a note above the fiddle. It was the kind of voice you couldn't imagine refusing. My heart skipped—not so much because a stranger was asking me to dance, but because I was scared to death about the steps.

"Can't," I said. See, nobody had ever taught us to dance, not the way they do in the country. I suppose maybe once upon a time Mama and Papa had danced, had known how to move their feet. But they'd lost the steps after so long being town folk.

"Sure ya can."

Next thing he pulled me up, led me to the middle of the floor with his arm at my waist.

"Ya let the fella lead," he whispered in my ear, his breath soft on my neck, and I let my feet follow his, gliding and tapping in among the other pairs, their faces shadowed from the bright bulb over the stage.

I glanced over his shoulder to see if my sister or my brother was watching but couldn't spot them anywhere. My face just inches from his fresh-shaven jaw, the smell of soap and a faint smell of sweat. I could feel the warm damp pressure of his arm through the light cotton of my dress, the gentle squeeze of his fingers on mine. A deep humming in his throat to the fiddler's lament, like it came from down in his chest.

My stomach was in knots, but after a while I stopped worrying so much about my feet making a fool of me. When the music slowed I was worrying instead how *I* must smell, wishing I'd washed with plain water and not the carbolic soap. But then the music swelled and sped up, all without stopping, and the floor filled again, couples joining and parting, people swinging on the arms of endless partners like machinery gone wild, the workings of a watch speeded up jig-time.

"Enougha that," he said as we pushed off to the side—I suppose he didn't know the steps either. "Wonder they don't bust through the floor," he laughed, leaning towards my ear, his hand still on my waist. "I'm not much for reels but I like the slow ones a'right."

I nodded, waiting for him to move off, and craned my neck looking for my sister again. The fiddler put down his instrument and went outside.

"Yer not expectin' anybody, I hope," he said as I caught a

flash of Mary Beth's skirt and glimpsed the fella with the wagon.

"No," I said, and he nudged me towards the kitchen, where he asked for two glasses of water.

"This is yer first time out here, ain't it?" He drank his water, then set the glass on the wooden counter, all the time staring at my hat. Next thing he whipped it off my head, to get a better look, I suppose, and twirled it on his finger.

"That's better," he said as I snatched it back. "You can't be from town either, or I'd a reco'nized ya. No, I don't b'lieve I've seen ya before—I'd remember if I had."

We found two chairs beside the stage, pushed over to let the fiddler climb back up. The music got so loud we couldn't talk. I finished my drink and held onto the glass, balancing it on my palm till he took it from me and set it under his seat. He rolled up his sleeves and sat with his arms folded, both feet pumping to the music, knees bouncing like the fiddler's. The two of us looking straight ahead, our arms just touching.

I saw Mary Beth and that fella go outside, and my brother Dan on the bench doubled over with a cigarette in his hand, nodding to the man next to him. After a while he saw me and came over.

"Tom Gillis?" he said, rubbing the side of his face.

"Thomas."

Then Dan, embarrassed, ignoring him: "Looks like we're gonna be walkin' home, girl." As if I were sitting there alone, my hands folded in my lap, the loose hairs tickling my forehead in a sudden draft of air.

"I can give the two of ya a ride," Thomas said. "Think I've had enougha this stuff for one night. After a while it starts soundin' the same."

He had a motorcar, one of the Model Ts parked along the ditch. Out in the warm darkness he took my elbow and helped me up to the running-board and into the back seat. My brother sat beside him up front.

The sky was dusty velvet with stars, not a light anywhere but fireflies sparking the spruces along the road, the whine of the fiddle growing fainter as we chugged along. Thomas didn't talk much, except to ask my brother's name and which section of the mine he worked in.

"I'm at the bankhead. Machine shop," Thomas said. "Old man got me the job." Even in the darkness I could see Dan stiffen. Dan, who quit school at fifteen to work underground, and never got himself a real trade. After that nobody spoke, except when Thomas asked where to let us off. Then he insisted in taking us down past the pithead and the washplant to the foundry, and our rowhouse across from the slag heap.

Dan got out first, without more than a nod, and as I was climbing down Thomas asked if he could see me again.

"I s'pose," I said, goosebumps coming up on my arms. I started to shiver from the damp wind off the bay. It got cool at night by the shore, especially with the foundry down to three shifts a week, like somebody'd pulled the plug on the red glow in the sky.

"Better get in before ya get cold," he said, a shine to his face from the streetlamp. "I'll come for ya Sa'rday night. Tell yer ma not to wait up, yer brother too. We'll take a drive, how's that?"

Dan wiping his feet in the doorway, watching us.

"A'right."

Anybody else, I'd have said I was busy. But his eyes looked so deep under the flickering light. So I went with him that Saturday night, and the next and the next. I'm not sure how it happened, but on the third night I let him kiss me, and things went from there like a trip racing down a shaft, nothing to do but hop out once you reach the bottom.

Next I knew I'd stopped bleeding. I kept my lip buttoned, too scared to mention a word of it to anyone. And out of the blue Thomas asked me to marry him. Just like that. Took me up to his home once or twice for dinner with his sister, Irene. Both his parents just dead—I suppose the fella was lonely. Not much company, his sister.

I hear the doctor's step at the back door, his low voice amongst higher ones, Mama's and Mary Beth's, a child's crying. The pain stops and I catch my breath, waiting for the next one. I roll onto my back, breathing so deeply the walls swim. I wait and wait but no pain comes. I roll back onto my side, the sheets drawn up to my chin. Mama comes upstairs, the doctor's heavy tread behind her. She's telling him about the bloody show, my water breaking. He comes in and sets his little bag on the dresser. I close my eyes, pretend to sleep, the mound of my stomach still under the quilt.

"False labour," he says, his hands on my belly.

"So soon after the other, nature's little reprieve," Mama tries to joke.

"Call me when it's time," the doctor sighs.

Downstairs I hear Thomas cursing the wasted visit, hear the crunch of footsteps in the snow. More crying, the kettle whistling like a siren.

September 1924. Thomas had a good job casting dies. My brother said the other men figured he'd be shop foreman someday. Truth was, they all thought he was too big for his britches. "That Gillis, he's all sugar or all shit," I heard Dan tell Papa once. "Young fella like that tellin' men twice his age what to do." Mary Beth didn't think much of him either, though I figured she was just jealous when the fella with the wagon snubbed her.

Mama and Papa seemed to like Thomas all right—anybody could see I'd done better for myself than they might've expected. "Find yerself a fella can give ya nice things, Harriet," Papa always said. Though I wonder now what difference that would make.

We had a proper wedding—you see, I was the only one

who knew. I never told a soul and, being so thin and slight, it was months before I started to show. You couldn't tell a thing. I never told Thomas, see, because by then I was scared he might change his mind. Especially as things with the company weren't so good, and there was talk going round about men losing shifts. Threats, too, about chopping wages.

We came right home from the church—I guess you could argue we took the honeymoon first. Thomas had a little bottle of rum somebody had given him, and he poured Papa a glassful while Mama and I had tea. Not a thing to eat in the house—not that I felt much of an appetite, the squeamish feeling in my belly lasting well into the afternoon most days. Still nobody knew, not a soul.

After Mama and Papa left, Thomas took my hand and led me upstairs, the place all musty and half-furnished from the last people who'd lived there. The bedroom was pink painted-over wallpaper, with a big yellow spool bed, just the bare mattress with feathers poking out of the blue-striped ticking. I think I could still hear Papa latching the gate as Thomas pressed against me, tugging at the buttons of my thin white dress, and the rustly sound of made-over silk. For a moment he waltzed me gently around the room, my bodice around my waist, as I pushed myself against him to keep covered up. Then, placing my arms at my sides, he laid me down on the bed, began rooting under my skirt, my chemise. The pressure in my belly spread lower, till I thought his weight would make me burst. And what had seemed so sweet in the dark of a meadow or beside a brook suddenly felt shameful, dirty somehow. No kissing or whispering, no gentle searching or prodding. Just his weight on my swollen breasts, his jagged breathing.

"Thomas," I said afterwards, kissing the mole on his neck. "I've got somethin' to say to ya."

After I told him he rolled off me and pulled up his trousers, the look of a wounded animal in his eyes.

"Bitch," he said, and I pretended not to hear. I ran downstairs to rinse my face and vomited into the toilet, letting the tap run. Then I changed into my polka-dot dress to go uptown shopping. He waited outside while I drifted up and down the aisles, choosing dishes and cutlery, a set of speckled pots, a winter's worth of sugar and flour.

"Better stock up now, me love," the clerk said, but I had no idea what he meant. Then Thomas came in and paid the bill, shouldering the sack of flour. He paid cash for everything, even the pots. I blushed as he counted out the money, so used to things going on Papa's tab.

"No bobtail paysheets for me," he said, dusting flour off his lapel as he piled things in the car. Then he took off his jacket and loosened his shirt—it was almost October but the leaves were just starting to turn. And something about our reflection in the shabby storefront made me smile, in spite of what he'd just done to me. Like any new bride, proud and anxious to please.

*

For a wedding present Thomas had his mother's pump organ moved down to our place from the big house uptown. His sister was barely speaking to me by then—I suppose this didn't help matters.

"Don't spend all day foolin' with that thing, now," he'd say on his way to the machine shop every morning. I'd laugh like it was all a lark. By then the sickness had passed, and as the days grew shorter and colder and the leaves started to fall mornings became my best time. I'd get the wash out once Thomas left at six, standing at the clothesline in the cold clear air, sometimes wiping off a slick of frost before I pegged on the clothes. With the damp, cold smell of ice from the north and the sun at that short slant, you didn't mind the fire on in the kitchen all day.

Once I'd got the wash out and tidied the kitchen, I'd make a cup of tea and take it with me while I washed and powdered myself. I'd take my time choosing my clothes, the top drawer of underthings scented with lavender from the satin sachet Mary Beth had embroidered for my wedding. I still had no trouble fitting into my dresses, though as the weeks passed I started leaving the waists unbuttoned, the gap covered by my apron. Even when I grew out of them and started wearing Mama's old smocks, and the heavy wool coat she'd cut down from an uncle's uniform, I still took the time to keep myself nice.

After I'd braided up my hair I'd go to the parlour and sit at the organ, fiddling with the keys. Pulling out the stops, pushing them in, memorizing the names on them in faded black script. Thomas's sister—in a fit of guilt, I suppose—had sent down an old hymnbook of their mother's. Perhaps she felt sorry for me, alone like her in the house all day, or else she just wanted to show me up, make me feel there were certain things beyond me.

By the time my belly started to show, I could play "Onward, Christian Soldiers" and "Rule, Britannia" from my head. And "Skye Boat Song" too, with both hands, the walls and floor shaking from all the pumping. As long as I was in my apron by noon, with the rest of the day to cook and bake and clean some more, so everything would be just right when Thomas came home at six.

"I want ya to listen to somethin'," I said one evening, after finishing up the supper dishes and putting the kettle on for Thomas's tea. It was a few days after Christmas; the windows were frosty black, there were no sounds from the frozen street but the far-off barking of dogs.

"Company wants to cut wages twenty per cent," he said, rocking back in his chair. "Wants to keep fellas like me outta the union in case there's a strike. So if the miners try to shut 'er down, we'll have to keep things goin', keep 'er from floodin'."

"Well, at least ya won't lose wages."

"The hell you know about it," he snapped, then loosened up a little, small and skinny as a youngster sitting at the table.

"What is it ya want me to hear, Het?" He sounded so weary—
I figured it must be his shifts making him tired.

"December's the worst—it'll get better once the days start
gettin' longer."

"I said, what is it ya want me to hear?"

I poured a cup of tea for him, thick and black the way he
liked it, stirred the milk and sugar around and around till it
was pale and sweet.

"Come upstairs," I said.

"You're disgustin'," he sneered, as if I were asking him to
come up to bed.

I went up to the parlour anyway, sat on the little horsehair
stool with my eyes closed and played my hymn. After a while
Thomas leaned in the doorway holding his cup.

"You got nothin' better to do all day than that?"

"All right for yer sister, though, I s'pose."

"That's different—Irene's *musical*. Far as yer concerned, Het,
too bad they don't put women to work in the mines. Seein' as
ya don't have enough ta keep ya busy around here."

After that I never played if Thomas was in the house. The
bigger I got, the harder it was anyway; by the end my belly was
so huge I couldn't pull the stool up close enough to reach the
pedals.

*

March 1925. That first time, the pains started when I was at
the clothesline, reaching up to peg Thomas's workshirt. It was
a grey March morning, the wind so fierce it snagged the clothes,
twisting them end over end, making the pulley screech. The
yard was covered in dirty ice—nothing had started to melt yet.
Dampness that would eat through your bones. I'd gotten so
big and clumsy it felt like my ribs would split, the baby's head
pushing on my bladder and little feet knifing my stomach.
The only good thing about it was that Thomas had been leaving
me alone, since Christmas anyway, spending longer and longer

hours at the bankhead and Lordy knows where else. So, anxious as I was to unload my burden, part of me would have stayed that way for ever, like a pendulum stuck in mid-swing.

At night Thomas would wait till he thought I was asleep to come to bed, my smock and apron folded over the chair for next day and me tucked under a pile of quilts in my flannel nightie. I'd lie still listening to Thomas snore, feeling the baby sway and lunge inside me like a fish. A big-eyed codfish pulled up from the bay, flapping its tail for dear life. And I'd pray somebody'd throw it back—throw the both of us back—so I'd never have to see it or hold it in my arms.

Thomas couldn't stand to look at me by then, I suppose. I guess it's hard for a man to find anything desirable in a woman in that condition. Though for me, I never stopped wanting him, wanting him in the *old* way.

*

Fella from the lumberyard next door went running for Mama and the doctor—must've seen me double over, half skidding off the icy step, wearing nothing but a flowered shift and a pair of shoes. He helped me into the kitchen, where I walked around in circles, not knowing what else to do. Like an animal in a pen, looking for a hole. When Mama came she put me to bed while we waited for the doctor, the big pains sweeping over me like breakers, tons of water rising and falling. From somewhere downstairs I could hear Thomas's voice, then the doctor coming in the back door, taking his time up the stairs. Poking and prodding me while I tore at Mama's hand, the sheets. Pain as sheer as a rockface, bursting, crushing the breath out of me. Then a scalding pain and the gush of blood and water, small blue limbs flailing in the doctor's arms, a tiny, squalling red face. His miserable wail, the first real time I'd heard a baby cry. And the wonder of such a thing coming out of my body, such strange flesh, stranger still because he was perfect.

But no Thomas. I suppose he stayed in the kitchen the whole time, till it was over. As Mama wiped blood off the tiny wrinkled scalp, I heard the crunch of tires in the yard and out the gate. He never laid eyes on the baby till Fulton was nearly a week old. God knows where he went—to his sister's maybe.

I had no time to fret about him. Every time worry crept into my head the baby would wind up to howl, that frail newborn cry, *a-waaaah, a-waaaah*. Pitiful, yet the sort of thing you'd draw blood or tear flesh to protect. Fulton wouldn't take the nipple at first and everyone fussed over that. Doctor said to give him water and once he got hungry enough he'd latch on. My milk came in and my bosoms got so heavy and hard I thought I'd burst, the blue veins standing out like rivers on a map, like a cow left too long to be milked. Eventually the baby started to suck, and by the time Mama left me on my own, the cracks on my nipples had begun to heal.

I was sitting by the stove nursing when Thomas came home. It was around dusk and I was starving—hadn't had a chance to make myself a bite or even a cup of tea. I was sitting there in the gloom, the baby pull-pull resting, pull-pull resting, his little cheeks working like bellows, his eyelids fluttering. So quiet I suppose Thomas thought maybe there was no baby after all.

He jumped when he saw us, looked away till I'd covered up, the little flannelette blanket draped over my breast.

"Miners are goin' on strike," he said, glancing around at the empty stovetop, the empty cutlery glass on the table. "Shut the whole works down, they will. Not a goddamn thing I can do but scab for the company. Them fellas'll kill me. But if they shut 'er right down, the whole town'll starve." He glared at the baby sucking so peacefully.

"Soon as he's asleep I'll get ya some supper, Thomas," I said.

He didn't seem to hear, but stumped upstairs to the parlour. When I heard the pages of a newspaper turning slowly, one by one, I crept upstairs with Fulton limp and warm on my shoulder and laid him in the little spool cradle by the bed. As I tiptoed to the landing Thomas shouted, "Bring me a cup of tea, Hettie. And a bite of somethin', too, while yer at it. Haven't had a thing all day, too goddamn nervous to eat, though Irene had a roast up at the house."

I ran downstairs to the pantry and rustled around, but the shelves were almost bare on account of the baby. Nothing but a piece of pie somebody left and a heel of bread. I made tea and took it up to him with the pie. Not taking his eyes off the paper, he started shovelling crust into his mouth.

"Gonna be grim, I can tell ya. Bloody grim." He never mentioned Fulton or me, or where he'd been the last seven days.

"It'll blow over," I said, hating the bitter look on his face. He dropped his paper and stared at me like the weight of the world was my fault.

"What the Jesus would *you* know?"

*

June 1925. My belly rumbled as I stood at the window with Fulton in my arms, the baby in just a diaper, the night being so sticky. His soft little limbs damp against my skin. A wakeful baby, but strong; he had no trouble by then holding his head up on his skinny little neck. It was like he knew something was in the air.

We'd been making do for a month or more with whatever bits of sugar and flour Mama could save for us. Though with no coal the foundry had been shut down, putting Papa out of work too. One of the neighbours had brought us a nice piece of cod they'd caught the day before. But we had no milk, hadn't had any for weeks, not even for our tea. And the coal in the shed was getting low—I thought Thomas should go out with Papa and Dan, and skim what he could off the crop behind the post office, like everybody else. But he wouldn't. *Belongs to the company, like everything else,* he said, which in a way I could've understood if he'd had just himself to consider. I didn't know what we'd do once the coalshed was empty. Pick coal off the beach, I guess.

Every now and then, while Fulton was napping, I'd open the square brown trunk by the dresser and look at my hat, the one Papa had bought me, and think what I might get for it, how much milk it would buy. Or the fancy lace curtain fluttering ever so slightly at the window in the muggy air. That is, if there was anybody to take them, or any place to buy milk. But no, the company had everything locked up tight, the whole of Blackett over a barrel.

It was milk I wanted more than anything. Sweet God, it was hard to keep putting it out, suckling the baby every half-hour it seemed, without putting something back. Not that he was suffering—a round, blue-eyed child with a wisp of Thomas's black hair, hair as fine as spider's silk. The feel of his buttery skin on mine would've been bliss to me, if I hadn't already felt my care being dragged from him to another. Mama said it couldn't happen while you were nursing. But I knew it already had, that there was more to the queasiness in my belly than hunger.

The soldiers had been out back since lunch-time, milling about like cattle on the tracks beyond the garden gate. All the afternoon they kept at it, banking sandbags, shouldering rifles, their horses rearing in the sultry heat. A moving field of khaki, they looked so hot in their jackets and britches, swords at their sides. So hot and thirsty a part of me would've asked some of them in for a drink of water. But for the knot of men on the far side of the tracks, drinking and shouting, getting ready to start hurling bottles. I'd heard Thomas leave at daybreak—I had no idea where he was.

After supper the mob got bigger, full of men drunk on rum and moonshine—silver, as they called it—smashing the bottles on the tracks and yelling insults, egging on the soldiers. I locked the back door and went upstairs to watch from the bedroom, hoping once it got dark the shouting would die down and I could get the baby to sleep. The poor mite, too little to know what the racket was about, but tuned to it somehow, fussy. Restless as the June bugs flicking at the window.

I put him down on the quilt, wiped some spit-up off his chin. His arms like windmills and legs kicking, fighting sleep. He started to wail and I picked him up again, his milky breath too warm on my neck.

A gunshot punctured the darkness, then the frightened roar of men's voices, the dusty drumming of hoofs. By the time I pushed the curtain aside the soldiers were gone, nothing but the bulk of empty coal cars standing on the tracks. Then a burst of orange lit up the sky beyond the station, flames leaping over the roof of the post office, shouts echoing through the roar and the far-off clanging of bells. "They've torched the pluck-me!" I heard someone yell as the glow turned to red, spreading through the darkness. Shadows were scurrying over the tracks, figures running with bundles and sacks over their shoulders, rolling barrels, kicking wheels of cheese. They staggered past the fence with their loot and in the porch-light I saw one man with a roll of linoleum on his back, another with a chest of drawers. In the glow I could see the desperate glee on their faces as they scurried through the trees, past stacks of lumber in the yard next door. Their muffled shouts drifted through the window and Fulton started to howl again. As I put him to my breast I couldn't stop thinking of the look on those men's faces and wondering where on God's earth Thomas could be. When the baby finally settled, I felt something move in my belly, fluttery as mayflies but unmistakable.

I lay Fulton in his cradle, his eyes small and luminous in the dark, watching me, wide awake. I went over and turned on the lamp on the dresser. Beside it was a photograph of Thomas and me in a thin silver frame, a picture of us in his car after our wedding, Thomas's face white and plain against his dark suit, me smiling in my white dress, so pale it was hard to tell where the dress ended and my skin began. Fulton started wailing again, the cradle lurching, his tiny fists punching the air.

I took the picture from its frame and went downstairs, holding it tightly while I checked the back door. At the stove I gave the embers a poke, folded the photo in half. I shoved it in, watching its edges etched red and shrivelling into ash like a wasps' nest. Then I went to the sink and filled a mug with water, gulping it down before dashing back up to the baby.

*

The doctor's tires spin for a moment on the ice in the driveway and Mama comes back upstairs with Fulton in her arms. She sets him down on the floor beside the bed and he pulls himself up, clinging to the quilt, clamouring for me.

"Mary Beth came with some biscuits. Before she left I got her to watch the baby while I put the diapers out. Are you a'right alone now or should I stay in case somethin' happens?"

"Where's Thomas?"

Mama lets out a sigh, her breath whistling through her bottom teeth.

"You never mind him now, Harriet. You hear me?" Then, in a softer voice, "He said somethin' about work, sure you'd think he'd be happier now he's workin' again. Bringin' in a good wage, too, Dan says, considerin'—"

There are rumours the company's in trouble after agreeing to take just ten instead of twenty per cent of the miners' wages. Thomas has been back to work since the summer, though his shifts have been cut in half.

"Don't leave me, Mama."

"Yer pa's gonna be wonderin' where his supper is, and it's just about time this fella was fed too," she says, grabbing Fulton as his skinny legs buckle. A cramp starts to swell at the bottom of my womb, the muscles of my belly clenching.

"Bloody excuse for a doctor," Mama says, settling into the straight chair by the bed. She takes my hand, stroking my wrist while Fulton stumbles and claws at her knees. "Don't worry, my girl, it'll be over before ya know it," she whispers, hoisting the baby and carrying him out.

Downstairs I hear her talking to the operator as the lids start clattering again on the stove. Another pain rises, and then another, so close together I barely have time to catch my breath, all knotted up in my chest. I make myself keep breathing, till my lungs push the pain back down to my womb. Blowing out in time for the next, like racing waves on a shoal. Till finally I give up and let them suck me under.

The Accident

*On Tuesday, December 6, 1938, twenty miners died in Sydney Mines'
Princess Colliery when a cable broke, sending their riding-rake crashing
down a two-mile slope. One more man died later in hospital. This disaster
happened a year to the day after an earlier accident that claimed three
lives. For many years after, Princess miners refused to work on that day.*

Hettie

I knew something was wrong that morning when Thomas came
home from the machine shop at quarter to seven. His hands
were as clean as when he'd left an hour before, but for a little
cut on his finger. It was dark as midnight, the five boys still in
their nightclothes squalling for breakfast, and as usual I was
trying to do half a dozen things, get the wash started while the
porridge cooked. Just a week to go before my time, I was on
my knees in the porch looking for mitts when Thomas came
in, his head down as if he were still out in the fog. Struggling
up to see who it was, I think I startled him—his face was like
tallow and he was out of breath. Didn't bother taking off his
pea-jacket, soaked with drizzle.

"Accident at the pit," he said, dropping his lunchpail. He
spoke in a whisper, so soft and calm I figured it was nothing
too serious—somebody's finger lost in a casting mould, or
perhaps a rockfall, a leg broken.

"Oh?" I grabbed the pot, started ladling out the oatmeal.
"Didn't hear a thing." Not a bump or a shout, nothing besides

the far-off whine of a siren, and I'd been up since five to make Thomas's lunch.

The boys clammed right up, quit kicking each other under the table. Picked up their spoons and started eating, forgetting to fight over the sugar.

"Man-rake let go," Thomas said, still in that queer, calm voice. He scraped his hair back, leaving a little red streak on his forehead, and licked his finger. "Whole trip outta control down the slope, cars piled up at the bottom every which way. They think a cable snapped."

"*Oh my Lord.*"

The kids stopped eating, milk splattering the cloth.

"Who, Pa? How many?" somebody blurted, I think it was Fulton. *My brother.* It ripped through me like lightning, a hot-cold flash. I dropped the pot, watched it wobble on the lip of the stove, watched Thomas shove it back.

When he finally spoke, his voice was so low I wanted to put my hands to his throat and drag it out of him.

"They dunno yet, 'cept it was a full trip, six-thirty shift goin' down, good two hundred men at least. Heard somebody say the chain runner was down below somewheres, fixin' wires, an' one a the men gave the signal to start 'er up. So nobody knows how many were ridin' the rake. Jesus knows who's down there."

"*Dan,*" I said, and Thomas put his hand on mine, as if covering up a sore. Then, knowing the kids were watching, he yanked it away, cleared his throat.

"Don't be foolish now, it was fellas from the day shift goin' down. Night shift washing up when it happened, safe and sound."

Thoughts beat around my head like a bird in a chimney as I tried to remember what exactly Mama had said about Dan taking the odd day once in a while so a buddy of his could see his kids. Being a bachelor Dan didn't care when he worked, though Mama liked him on days so she didn't have to pussyfoot around while he slept.

Dan.

Thomas saw my confusion and twisted me by the elbow into the rocker. I sat there trying to collect myself, the kids all eyes, their porridge going cold.

"A year to the day, too, after that last one—remember those three, that fella and his son and the other. . . ." The colour rose in his face as he gave my shoulder a rough little clap. "And they say lightning don't strike twice—" He stood by the stove with his fists in his pockets, jumpy in a way I'd never seen him. Yet so quiet I wanted to pound him with my fists.

Danny.

Then he buttoned his coat, yanking the collar up as he went back outside. I made the boys throw their boots on over their bare feet, coats on top of their pyjamas. Didn't stop to take off my apron or to scrape the porridge back into the pot. Just grabbed my coat, did up as many buttons as I could and ran after Thomas, already way ahead up the tracks. The boys scrambled behind me through the gate after him, joining the stream of women and kids stumbling towards the pit, some in their nightdresses, carrying babies. Shouts rang out through the fog, but no crying—tears would have slowed us down.

Near the shaft came more shouting, a crowd hunched together blue-faced in the cold drizzle, the ground shining wet. Stinking of burnt metal, the fog echoed with the clang of shovels. We pushed closer as draegermen hoisted on their gear and disappeared down the black hole, Reverend Capstick standing back as two strangers in suits spoke to some men. I recognized them—buddies of Dan's from the night shift, still in their pit clothes.

Dr. MacLellan was there, and nurses from the hospital in North Sydney, dragging blankets and bandages off a truck. In the fog they looked like seagulls in their white uniforms and dark capes, their arms tucked up underneath.

I looked for Mama—by then word must have reached that part of town. Though lately she'd been finding it hard to get her breath, I knew she'd have hurried had Dan been at work.

It's all right, he can't be down there, I told myself, the blood thumping in my ears. *He's home sleeping, otherwise Mama would be here. Wouldn't she?*

Slowly the draegers came out in pairs, carrying stretchers—one at a time at first, then more and more, laying them in rows on the ground. Dozens and dozens of men, some not moving, bleeding from wounds so bad I couldn't look. The crowd hushed up, the moans coming from those stretchers enough to snap your nerves. I tried counting, then gave up.

A man, his face a sooty mask, limped from the pit and the crowd lunged forward, and then another came out, both of them bent and shaking, their teeth chattering. The first had blood running from a slash over his eyes, the other was still clutching his pit can.

"Holy Jesus," a shout went up, then a buzz of voices.

"One Christly mess down there, nothin' but bodies an' torn-up metal, cars smashed so bad you'd hardly reco'nize 'em."

The man with the lunchbox started weeping.

"Miracle anybody survived, a goddamn *miracle*," said the other, as a woman lunged out and threw her arms around him, blood and soot all over her soggy apron.

Fellas jumpin' over the sides like flies—

S' help me God, I jumped out before she hit that curve—

Poor poor buggers hardly had time to think—

Both men weeping, the crowd moving back. A woman looking to be in my condition bent down and brought up her breakfast.

Then I saw Thomas and some others in their shirt-sleeves and suspenders going in with shovels. *My brother.* I tried picturing him in bed at Mama's, his face slack and pink with sleep. Wouldn't let myself think of him down there in that black rubble, lost.

Some more men stumbled out, one smiling crazily, his eyes glittering through the soot, one with his hand gone, blood soaked like tar into his clothes. Another crawled on his hands and knees and wanted to know what time it was. And all the time the crowd kept growing, people stamping their feet to keep warm, their voices hardly a murmur.

By eleven o'clock they started bringing out stretchers covered with tarpaper. I drew a big breath, my hands over my mouth, the crowd dead silent. One of the stretcher-bearers saw me and stopped.

"I'm sorry for ya," he said, touching the peak of his pit helmet, his eyes looking over my shoulder. Through the coal dust I saw he was one of the night men. "Poor poor Dan. Musta been one a the first to go, always so anxious to start work."

I felt the baby drop, the wind being sucked out of me. Someone gripped my elbow and I could feel Thomas come up and shove the children away. Heard him yell at the oldest ones to watch the others, mind they didn't get in the way. Then he came and stood beside me.

"At least they got 'im out in one piece. Others weren't so lucky," he said, reaching out to lay his hand on my shoulder. I twisted away.

"Lucky," I choked, watching Dan's friends carry the stretcher to the wash-house.

"Ya better have a look, Hettie, make sure it's him," Thomas said, wiping sweat off his face. I turned, the tears thick, and grabbed for the kids, their frozen hands. Without a word they followed, sticking close as I stumbled from the pit yard to the roadway. Somehow I made it down to Mama's, my eyes to the ground, watching my feet carry me. Taking in every rock and pebble but hardly seeing.

Papa was helping Mama down the steps when we got there, a neighbour waiting for them in his car. The look on her face was terrible, grey as her shabby coat and the dusty veiled hat she'd put on, her hair matted and flat from her pillow. She breathed in deep when she saw me, then looked away, her arm trembling up from her cane, and leaning so heavy on Papa I thought the two of them would stumble in the mud. The rain had gotten thicker, beading everything with ice.

"Company says it's him," Papa said, his fist to his mouth.

"They want us to identify—"

Mama closed her eyes and covered her face with her hands.

"Fellas in the machine shop s'posed to check that cable," Papa said, his chest heaving, his eyes like stone.

"*James!*" Mama cried, falling against him. "I have to go to him, I have to know." She looked at me. "There's always the chance—"

"Mama," I said, my face against her coat, the smell of liniment and camphor.

"Blamin' people won't bring him back," she wailed, raising her head. Then she clenched her jaw. "You get those kids to school, and while you're there tell your sister. Tell Mary Beth to go to the pit, if she's not there already. Then go on home, Harriet. Nothin' ya can do, save tellin' Mary Beth."

The neighbour got out and helped them into his car and they drove off, leaving me and the kids on the porch. I was tired from walking, weighed down by wet clothes, but somehow we made it back uptown to the Grey school, the boys running ahead. In such a rush, though when we got there the school was half empty, kids run off at recess to follow the sirens, I suppose. But Mary Beth was there—through the pebbly window I could see her shape at the blackboard. I knocked and she opened the door a crack, grimacing as though she already knew what I'd come for. When I told her she swallowed hard, her eyes brittle as she shut the door behind her and put her hands over her face. Waiting outside the staffroom while she got her coat, I expected her to cry or even curse. But she didn't say a thing.

*

Four days later they buried Dan, him and nineteen others including a couple of men down the street from us, a father and his son. Another died in hospital a few days after that, suffering terribly from his injuries, they said. That helped me some with losing Dan—the fact that it was over for him so quick, that maybe he hadn't known what hit him. And yes, that at least we had him to bury—the end, someone said, of Dan's quick thinking. One fella who made it said when they felt the cable snap some of the men stretched out stiff in their little cars while others started jumping, sparks and parts of bodies flying up from the runaway wheels. Said that's what saved a few, lying down straight like that, like riding bobsled. A few, that is, except for Dan.

Even at the funeral parlour I couldn't bring myself to look at him, though everyone said he just looked like he was sleeping. So pale and young, the coal dust scrubbed off his face. Thirty-six years old, no widow or children to leave behind. Just a boy, Mama wept, just a boy.

Dan had been buried a week when my sixth child came, on a dismal morning like the day of the accident—such queer weather for December, so close to Christmas yet nothing but rain. The baby bore no resemblance at all to my side of the family. Still, Thomas never blinked at the name I picked: Daniel MacCallum Gillis, after the baby's uncle. And I made up my mind never to mention the cable, though for a long time Thomas seemed like he was waiting for me to bring it up, maybe even wishing I would. Until the company had a section of it tested by experts and declared the accident an act of God, and we tried our best to forget.

*

Mary Beth

It fell upon me to make the arrangements. I board uptown, you see, a block from the funeral parlour, so it only made sense. I've always been good at organizing and making plans, in a way the rest of my family seems incapable of. Especially Harriet, with her ever-expanding brood and little or no help from her husband, from what I can see. No, the odd thing is that my brother and I were the capable ones, and with him gone, naturally things got left up to me. Proper thing, I suppose, as it's helped take my mind off the accident, allowed me to keep a grip on myself, a degree of decorum, so *lacking* in the others.

It's important for my pupils, for one thing, that I keep a rein on my feelings. Particularly those children who lost fathers. Yes, tragedy is one thing—but to resort to public hysteria is to insult the dead, I've always thought. And my dear brother would have agreed, I'm certain.

I requested a mid-priced casket of polished oak—was adamant about helping Papa pay for it from my meagre salary. Small sacrifice for a loved one, I said. I arranged all the flowers as they arrived at the visitation room, a bouquet of white carnations from the company and a wreath from the union. I made sure that my brother's suit was pressed and that he was perfectly shaven. Morbid, some might say, macabre. But I felt it my duty, especially for Mama's sake, and in this town one can never trust others to carry things out to the letter. Not the way one would do oneself.

Mr. Cameron, the principal, kindly offered to take the grade fives for the remainder of the week, until the men were buried. I would have preferred to continue teaching, to keep myself occupied and also as a model for the students, but decided it would appear unseemly. Having the children spell "beautiful" and "jubilant" while my brother lay dead, drilling them on times-tables, borrowing and taking away. Worst of all would have been the curiosity on their pale round faces, watching for a chink in my demeanour. Even the ones themselves bereaved, grieving for loved ones—they would all be watching, their scrutiny like salt in a wound. Oh yes, children can be cruel. Particularly embittered ones, children already hardened to life's sad experience. So I suppose it was as much for me as for my brother's memory that I accepted Mr. Cameron's offer; I believed some time away from the classroom assured me of keeping my head, and having my brother meet his rest as unbesmirched in body and reputation as I knew he was in spirit.

"Take as long as you need," Mr. Cameron said, patting my

hand in the staffroom that awful morning. His generosity I found embarrassing, but nothing compared to Harriet's snivelling in the hallway. She looked like death warmed over, soaked to the skin and her stomach fit to bursting, the hem of her coat hiked up in front.

"There's been a death in the family," I told him, speaking in deep measured tones so as not to elicit more attention than could be helped. Then I put on my coat and stepped into the hall, ushering my bedraggled sister away before she created more of a scene. Whimpering and choking like a child, half out of her head with grief. I bit my lip until it bled, but I would not cry. Not a single tear, at least not in public view. Thank the Lord, when we got outside she said she was going home and I ran ahead without any more to-do, mud splattering the backs of my stockings as I dashed towards the pit yard.

It was like a scene from the Great War—the ground dotted with first-aid stations and rows of stretchers, fog swirling around the tops of the buildings, the air heavy with the smell of scorched wire. And another odour, like the inside of my brother's pit can when he left it for Mama or me to wash. *The earth's guts,* he would tease, though he claimed he couldn't smell it himself.

Outside the wash-house I spied my parents talking to the minister, their heads bowed as he prayed with his hands on their shoulders. He opened his eyes and reached for my hand as I drew near, the rain like an icy veil between us.

"Not my brother," I said, putting my arms around Mama, holding her as Papa twisted his cap in his hands. Reverend Capstick shrugged, raising his eyes to the pulleys and cables atop the shaft as if waiting for some divine response.

The worst, of course, was yet to come, and nothing prepared me for what I went through next—the *rage* I felt as a bald man from the company led us inside the wash-house and drew back the sheet of tarpaper from my brother's face. The way Mama crumpled to her knees, like a ball of paper in a fire, and kissed his cheek. I helped her up, forcing myself to think of other things—square roots, equations. The total of absentees each day on the roll-call. And that's how I got through it, by simple arithmetic. Arithmetic, and my knack for organization.

I left my parents then and made my way directly to the funeral parlour, took care of all the arrangements straightaway. Unbearable to have one's flesh and blood laid out cold and dirty on a washroom floor, like something lost or discarded. At the visitation the following night I heard somebody mention how clean my brother looked, not a trace of his livelihood on his body, or a hint of his misfortune. Cold comfort, but a kind of vindication too, for all of us but Harriet. She refused to look.

*

The day of the funeral we had freezing rain. It fell on the procession, coating windshields with a pebbly slick of ice that made it hard to see. I accompanied my parents in their neighbour's car, following the long line of hearses as they wound along Main Street past the school. In the windows I could see the students, the few who hadn't lost a relative in the accident, lining up to watch. It was a dark, dismal morning; the lights were on in the classrooms, bright yellow globes in the fog. I glanced up at my room and thought for a second I saw Mr. Cameron, a tall shape among the smaller ones pressed against the glass. I believe he waved to me but I turned quickly, clasping Mama's hand as encouragingly as I could. And so we buried my brother, one of many families huddled together that day in the rain-swept cemetery. And on the following Monday morning I returned to school, giving myself an extra hour before the bell rang to get caught up.

I didn't like what Mr. Cameron had done in my absence— rearranged the strap and the piles of notebooks on my desk, left a stack of work uncorrected. I was at my desk marking sums when he came to my classroom; I planned to drill the children in math first, then spelling.

I could see his face behind the mottled glass, hesitating,

perhaps afraid to disturb me. He rapped at the door before he stepped in, his hands in his pockets, the top of his head shiny pink through his thin grey hair.

"I'm sorry about your brother, Miss MacCallum," he said, the shoulder of his jacket brushing the chalkboard. I continued marking—borrow one, carry two.

"I'm sorry about Dan," he said again, and I dropped my red pencil. I watched it roll to the floor, bouncing off the eraser. Mr. Cameron bent to retrieve it, rolling it between his palms before he set it on the blotter.

"Are you *quite* sure you're ready to be back?" he asked, and I felt my cheeks flush. I resumed marking, ticking off the answers with neat red marks, snapping the crinkled pages.

"Well," he sighed, "don't be surprised if attendance is poor. The children will no doubt be a little restless still."

"Mr. Cameron?"

I am and have always been a stickler for discipline, a firm believer in the adage that one only reaps as much as one sows.

"I just mean go easy on them, Miss MacCallum. Some are bound to be upset."

"Of course," I said, scraping my chair back as the bell sounded. I rose and followed him to the door, eyeing the dusty swath on his sleeve.

"Don't hesitate to let me know if you reconsider—I quite enjoy taking a class from time to time. That is, if you feel you need more time—"

I smiled and shook my head as my pupils started filing in, filling up the rows of desks. Waiting for them to be seated I opened the arithmetic book, drew a fresh piece of chalk from my drawer, then stood at the board while they settled.

"The square root of twenty-five?" I called, the book pressed to my bosom. One of the girls raised her hand, stood up timidly at her desk, rubbing her frayed cuff.

"Josie?" Then I noticed the scrap of newspaper in her hand.

"It's a poem," she said, spots of colour rising to her cheeks. "I was wondering if I could—" The rest of the class stopped fidgeting, put down their pencils. I felt my face go hot.

"I think that unnecessary—" I began, but the child remained standing, her gaze steady. "Well, I suppose it can't do any harm," I hedged, their eyes upon me. "Go ahead, but be quick."

Her eyes fixed on the board, she began reciting in a small wavering voice:

The cable snapped, the boxes jarred,
Then faster spun the wheels,
The runaway cars plunged down the deep,
While death raced at their heels.
Some leaped, and luckily, saved their lives,
Before it was too late,
While others fell beneath the wheels
And fearful was their fate. . . .

I held my breath and focused on a tree in the window as she went on and on, lingering over the rhyming words as if it were a lullaby. And when at last I thought she was done, the girl began reading names, the names of all who had been lost. I braced myself for my brother's, and when it came I stared hard at the grey limbs, the dull bark against the glass, until another small voice whispered, "*Daniel MacCallum!* That's the one who filled in for my pa!"

I picked up the strap then, brought it down hard on the side of the desk. The girl fell quickly to her seat; their stunned faces were a blur as I rushed from the room, slamming the door behind me.

I started to cry then, leaning against the coats in the hallway, the smell of wet wool a queer comfort.

Dan, I told myself. *To me he was Dan.*

After the Angel Mill

Blackett, 1940

It's been three days since James got out of bed last—come all
the way downstairs, wouldn't take no help. Had to see if his
legs still worked, is what he said. Had to go out back for a whiff
of air. He gets so tired, laying up in that bed all day; he's been
up there since the first big blizzard in January, and here it's
pushing spring. I'm sure he wishes I could read to him—he
hasn't the strength to hold a book. But both of us knows it's
no sense wishing for what you can't have.

When he said he was getting up, nothing I could do but
follow, ready to grab him by the collar if his legs give out on
the stairs. Lot of good that would've done, likely landed the
two of us in a heap at the bottom. But maybe, Lord help me, it
would've been for the best.

He's failing, I knows it, but I'm not ready to think it, not
yet, for thinking makes it so. It's like my head won't give in to
what's there in my heart. Besides, we all knows how sure the
heart is—about as sure as blue sky for a picnic.

I watched him make it to the kitchen, one hand on the
wainscot like a blind man feeling the way, the other on his
cane. When he got to the back door he waited, gasping in and
out to get his breath as I undid the bolt and threw my shawl
over his shoulders.

A jeezly cold day for April. I thought the wind would knock
him down when I opened the storm-door, the two of us

shivering out there on the stoop watching the ocean. Nothing but whitecaps and chunks of ice like giant teeth, and the wind! Wind as cold as Greenland.

"It's good," James said, hanging onto his cane, his head laid back against the shingles. "Does a fella good." He had his eyes shut, gulping the air like it was something to drink, though you could see how each breath pained him. The wind near ripping the sheets off the line, whipping a bit of colour into his cheeks. First I'd seen in months, since the doctor told him to rest.

"That's enough, man," I said, laying my palm against his face, the white prickles of his beard. Underneath the skin was burning. Then he started coughing, like the air had gone down the wrong way. Coughed so bad he doubled over and I had to help him inside, where he sat at the table till he caught his breath.

A new linen cloth I'd just laid there—Mary Beth gave it to me for my birthday. I couldn't look at what he'd brought up, half the poor man's lungs I swear. I bunched it up and left it while I got him back upstairs to bed. When I come down again I put it in the cellar to soak, Mary Beth's handiwork and all. I still don't have the gumption to wash it.

That was the last time he got up, which makes me think he won't be lingering much longer. I see a restlessness even when he sleeps, as if my James is anxious now to be on his way, as if it's time he was moving again. Lord knows we've been here longer than anyplace else, longer than either of us could've imagined, once. It's where we've gotten old, though funny thing, when I look out over the clift and see those miles and miles of ocean I don't think of this as home, even after forty years. But James does—he's stubborn, like them spruces out near the edge, bent and puny from the wind and spray but clinging like barnacles to the rocks.

Which is why it's so hard to believe he's going now. Through thick and thin he always had his health, never missed a day at the mill. Until we lost Dan in the pit—that knocked the stuffing out of us, it did, me as much as James. I knew I'd not get over it—but James? It's like all the bad things started catching up with him then, like a pack of dogs chasing the fish-man, jumping up and biting the bejeezus out of him. But me, I've been the type never bothered trying to outrun them in the first place, just kept apace with things and prayed they wouldn't take too big a piece of me. So long as I had James, see, it seemed I could always keep a little bit ahead. Though when Dan died it threw me back, way back to them things like curs howling by the side of the road, waiting to spring.

*

Acadia Mines, Colchester County, 1894
We'd only been out a few months before we lost our first one, just long enough to get settled. By that I mean blankets on the bed and a good-sized woodpile. Thank the Lord there was a place waiting for us when we got there, a little rust-red house with a patch of garden past the iron mine and the blast furnace. Not what you'd call a *home* exactly, but as much as the company would allow. A roof over our heads, a table to eat off. And a damn sight better than what we'd left in England, a two-room rowhouse with not an inch of ground. James got $1.65 a day charging the coke ovens, better than a slagger or boilerman. Good money, back then.

But nothing prepared us for winter, though, no amount of saving or laying by. When little Albert took sick we were so numb we hardly knew what was happening, even when the doctor come in the middle of the night and told us not to hope.

Like a dream now, nearly fifty years past, that day in January we buried him. *Seven years old.* Gravediggers said lucky it wasn't a week or two later or the ground would've been hard as pig-iron. It was so cold the wheels of the wagon creaked, the sky so grey and still the horse's breath hung like fog. Just James and me and Joseph, our other young one, five or six years old, his eyes big and solemn in his small face. The parson's voice soft and muffled as he said a quick prayer over the little coffin, *Our Father who art in heaven,* spiky trees behind him like a wall and nothing but the far-off hiss and roar of the rolling mill by the creek.

As we drove off it started to snow, big soft flakes like feathers dusting the firs, like Somebody laying a blanket over us, saying *Rest now, rest.* That's what I wanted to do: lie down on the frosty ground and go to sleep. But I had work to do, and we'd only just arrived. So there was nothing to be done but keep going. Going and going—life's like that, though we all knows what we're headed towards.

It took two weeks to get here. We sailed from Bristol the tenth of August and it wasn't till the twenty-fifth we reached Canada, so sick of salt and deep black swells that the sight of land—any land—was a blessed gift. Even the granite shore with its strange scrub forest thick to the water's edge. So jeezly long coming across—to this day I knows that's what weakened Albert, sucked the boy's strength right out of him. And even now, so many years later, I tell you, if I'd a known my firstborn would be the price of passage, I'd have stayed put. Come hell or high water I'd have moved not a foot from the west country, the old country where I was born and my parents and grandparents before me. Never mind that the wool mills were closed and the ironworks shut down—James and me would've made out somehow. And my Albert would've lived, yes, to a good age. Poor wee lamb, his little limbs so straight and thin, his face white as mortar. *Diphtheria,* the doctor said. But I knows it was them weeks at sea.

An awful thing, laying a child down. Except that in this new land he has a tombstone. In the old country he would not. And Lord knows what he's been spared—travail and tribulation, a lifetime's worth.

Not that living's all a vale. Oh no, it has its posies too. And in that time since losing Albert—now but a sprite in an old woman's dream!—we've lived another life, have James and I, in another place with other children.

Some years after Albert died, the works in Acadia Mines ran into trouble—oh, it was a crazy business, the price of iron like a seesaw every time you turned around, James could tell you more about it than me. Word come out the company was building a big new mill on Cape Breton Island, all the latest gadgetry. James and me hardly heard of the place before, except from some of the ore men James knew who said that's where the big mines were, the coal mines, and the money too. Place to be, they said. So when the company up and said they was sending him there, by God James was glad of it. Figured it could be no worse than Acadia Mines, no more than a patch in the woods without the works.

So in 1902 a bunch of us left what we'd started and took the train to this island, so James and the other men could start work on the new mill. He was proud, I knows, that they asked him to go. Nine years in that other place was enough for me— I hated to leave Albert, of course, the little plot in the Church of England cemetery. But since his death I'd got nothing but bad luck. Three more lost before my times were even up, and a little girl who lived no more than a couple of days. *Place was cursed*, I told James. So we didn't waste no time getting out, as far as that goes. And once we'd gone didn't word come that the mill there closed down altogether, and overnight the place become a ghost town. *Cursed*, I said, thanking our lucky stars we got out in time. And years later, swear to God, didn't a big fire come and burn the whole place to the ground, the ruined mill, the empty hotels, shops and houses. The Anglican church with its big white steeple, Albert's grave in the churchyard—a tangle of trees now, I s'pose. Pains me to think of him lying alone there but no, I've never gone back. Never have and I never will, not now, not without James.

For once we reached Blackett I said, *That's it, I ain't moving no more.* But it weren't for love of the place, I can tell you. I was carrying Dan and every step made me nervous as a cat, I was that afraid of losing him. We come in early autumn, already the trees were bare though from where they put us you'd hardly know the difference. A string of red rowhouses by the seashore, acrost from the new works. Not a decent-sized hardwood to be seen, nothing but alders and stubby spruce, and men working like dogs to get the ovens and furnaces going. Three years to build that mill, James and our young fella Joseph working night and day, the rest of the men from up the road too. The Capsticks on one side of us, the Aspinalls and the Cockells on the other with their big crowds of kids, lines and lines of washing flapping in the yards. The noise and commotion was something terrible, and me with three babies!

Yes, my luck changed once we got to Blackett, maybe it was the ocean air. That first November Dan was born, the next year Mary Beth and Harriet the year after that. But what I remember most is the noise, the clanging of hammers and steel outside, the squalling of chillern in the house. When it got too much I'd go out back and look at the mountains in the distance, on a clear day like the backs of big green-and-purple cats sloped into the water. And always the wind, a sharp salt breeze off the sea, even with the rotten-egg stink of the mill. After a while I got a garden growing out back, tough things that don't mind the wind. Pink phlox and golden glow, sweet rocket and lupins, the peppery smell blowing through the house of a fine evening.

Joseph, then a big strong fella of sixteen, would come in from work with his father, James happy as a coot though worn to the bone. He said the mill was the biggest and best in all the Dominion of Canada, he never mentioned England. But then neither of us did, we were too busy. Too busy to notice much besides whatever needed doing that moment, till one day Joseph up and said he was taking a coal boat to Montreal. Next we got a postcard from the Boston States, a picture of a big building addressed to us in a queer hand. A stranger's hand, said James.

A year or two later a fella told James he'd met a young Joe MacCallum drunk as a dog on a ship out of New York City, but we never did find out if what the fella said was true or if it was our boy he'd seen. And that was the last we ever heard of Joseph, lost to us as our first one. Except I likes to think he's still alive somewhere, maybe down in America.

"It's the MacCallum in 'im," I said to James just after we heard that fella's story. "In his blood, I guess. Born restless, like you."

It was around the same time James started taking up reading—books, papers, maps—whatever he could get his hands on, every night by the fire when he was too tired to do much else. Where he got these things I don't know, maybe from one of the bosses at work. It was as if he thought reading would take him to Joseph, like cracking the code to the company's safe.

"Hmmmmph," he said. "Better he'd done his travellin' in his head!"

I jabbed my finger with the needle, a drop of blood staining the little lace collar I was working. I sat there trying to rub it off, wondering what was coming next.

"Long as 'e can sign his name he'll be a'right."

It was the cruelest thing he could've said—we both knowed Joseph was no book-learner, not by any stretch, but now I could see James was blaming *me*.

"And what has that got to do with anyt'in'?" I cried. All the years I'd gotten along fine without books—James never made no fuss. What did reading and writing have to do with birthing babies and cooking and cleaning and cutting down clothes to dress them all? A mother's love?

"Ya could've learned, Sarah—ya still could learn, if ya wanted to."

And in all our married life those were his bitterest words to me. For days after I wouldn't speak. Couldn't. See, it weren't my fault. In Wiltshire where I grew up, there weren't time for learning. My father, Samuel Elkins, was a labourer, my mother Lizzie a clothworker at the Angel mill. I had a couple of years' schooling, though you couldn't see much point in it. *She's already sharp as a tenterhook*, my parents said. And so at twelve I went into service for the ones who owned the mill, and there I stayed till I met James. Such a clever young man, hardly a trace of the brogue though his people came from Glasgow. An ironworker, a man with a trade who could also read and write his name—and mine too. Used to hold my hand with the chalk in my fingers, guide it round and round on a piece of slate, making little loops and curls. 'Course I went along with it, a kind of a lark. I think my people was a little afraid of him, his Scotch blood maybe, though he was never anything but gentle. But I could see no point in it—writing, I mean—and when we signed the register I made my mark with a cross. I was nineteen. A year later I had Albert, and I got along just fine thank you, just fine indeed, until the chillern got older and James started taking to books.

Then if I had a bit of time on my hands I'd try sitting for a spell with the Book of Common Prayer. It was the one thing James never looked at, so I could get it down and never worry about him missing it. Or worse, asking what was in it. For James was like that, 'specially after Joseph disappeared, wanting to know what you were doing, checking up. Not in a nasty way, but just to let you know he was in'erested.

I never looked at the prayer book when Dan and the girls were around. After Joseph I was more careful about keeping my problem from them. Foolish, of course, since chillern always knows a hun'erd times more than what we credit 'em for. But I was scared of having it rub off, and all of them such quick learners. Or so James said, after they'd stop to see him by the cooling pond on their way home from school. He'd give them each a peppermint for every poem they could recite.

I didn't make much headway, though. A minute here, a minute there, with the prayer book open on my lap in front of the fire. I always waited till the chillern were asleep and James upstairs getting washed. How those dim lines and squiggles would crawl on the pages, like specks of dirt and rows and rows of little bugs. And though I recognized some of the letters,

I could make no sense of it a-tall, the stack of pages as thick as my wrist. Then one night Mary Beth got out of her bed and come downstairs, and when she seen me sitting there she said, *Oh Mama, why are ya readin' it upside down?* And that was the end of me fussing with that business.

*

I'm up with James all the time now, his breathing's gotten so hard and raspy. My girls are downstairs, Hettie chasing wee Danny, trying to keep his holy terror out of mischief, and Mary Beth straightening up the kitchen for me. I'd rather they wouldn't try to help—last time Mary Beth come around it was another week before I put my hands on my measuring cup again, she likes to sort and tinker so. But she means well and James wants them here, not that he can get much rest with that little fella tearing around, knocking things over. Maybe the ruckus makes him feel better, or maybe he's past minding it. And maybe it's a good thing having a young one in the house at a time like this; he give us all a good laugh now and then, like the time he snuck out with the bedpan on his head. Takes your mind off the sick.

James is so weak now you can hardly tell if he's awake or sleeping. There's a cup of tea by the bed with a thimbleful of brandy in it for his strength. He stirs a bit in the bed and I put down my darning and hold out the tea, try spooning it to him a little at a time. His lips are dry and parched-looking as salt fish.

"Bahhh," he says, "I don't want none of that."

It startles me, this burst of will, and a bit of tea slops over onto the coverlet. Then James sinks into the pillow again, a grey shadow against the bedding. I reach for the plate Hettie's fixed, try feeding him a bit of cheese, a crumb of bread.

"Take it away," he says. I wipe the sweat off his face with my hanky.

"You got to eat somethin'," I coax. But my heart's not in

—47—

it. It never was any good going against him, like a trout fighting its way upstream.

"I'm gonna call Dr. MacLellan now," I say, and he half lifts himself off the pillow.

"That fella's a horse's arse," he croaks, and then he starts to laugh, a choking rattle down low in his chest.

"Bring me a pint," he says.

"Ya know there's no nourishment in that, James." He seems to lift himself higher in the bed.

"Get me a pencil then," he whispers, his voice no more than a wheeze. I grab the basin, hold it up by his mouth. He knocks it away.

"A pencil, Sarah, and a bit of paper."

There's a queer wetness in his eyes, a strange gleam.

"Doctor says not to bother yerself, James."

"Goddamn him, Sarah. I wants to put something down."

When I come back he's half sitting up. I prop a piece of scratch paper on one of his books, close his fingers around the pencil. But he don't seem to need my help, the soft scritch of lead moving acrost the page.

When he's done he shuts his eyes and lays back.

"Give it to Mary Beth," he says, so I take it downstairs. Mary Beth wipes off her hands on my apron, then picks it up and reads out loud:

Shore Row, Blackett, C.B.
April 24, 1940
My dear Son Joseph, the weather it is fine but still cold, much ice yet off of the harbour. I am pretty sick now and my breath it is short but last Tuesday I did go down to the back door for a little fresh air it was so lovely but the wind off of the ice. Your Mam and me have missed you Son but very soon I am coming to find you I hope that you will come home with me. X Your Pa X

Then she folds it in two and goes to the black case she

keeps her schoolwork in, starts rooting around for something. Finally she finds what she's looking for, an old manila envelope from someone's report card, and sticks the letter inside. With it tucked under her arm she stands over me and rubs my sleeve.

"There there, Mama," she says, "Don't you mind that foolishness now." Then she reaches behind me for her bag and drops the envelope in.

Resurrection

He was unblemished, perfectly preserved; there was no evidence of murder, no sign of sickness or mauling by ravenous animals. No horror registered in the iceman's stare, dead fish eyes shrivelled and dinted as dried grapes. His bones were intact, like tent-poles supporting a sagging tarp of tawny rawhide skin: the temple of a soul.

The dwindling warmth of his body had melted a tomb in the falling snow, out of reach, and, blanketed, shrouded and buried, he had slept through five millennia—a Rip van Winkle in his icy grave, surviving thousands of thaws and freeze-ups. A small copper-bladed axe lay beyond the curl of his frozen fingers, dead flesh reaching for this amulet of survival. Death defied, considering the body's survival—as a shell if not a temple.

I adored the iceman the minute I saw him in the *Digest*, marvelled at his miraculous emergence, a resurrection, rivers of ice melting, nature conspiring to yield him up. In spring there's no telling what the earth will heave up, new crops of stones in the rocky ground. This year it's a body, a perfectly preserved traveller from the Copper Age. The *Digest* says he's five foot two with narrow shoulders and dark, wavy hair, dressed in skins stitched together delicately. By whose hands? So much care—the care of a woman? The final exhumation is botched by modern men wielding shovels, desperate to pry him from the glacier, so anxious to save his body that they mangle the lovely tunic and gouge away the testicles.

Just like people, I think. Then the dull thud of Ellen stumping up to the doorbell, and I remember I've invited her. I tuck the *Digest* under a stack of others piled on the coffee table, to protect him from her needling eyes. As she holds her swollen finger to the buzzer, I flit about the kitchen, wiping milk from the lip of the creamer, piling sugar-cubes just so in the little silver bowl, dusting off the Royal Albert. I like things to be nice even when it's Ellen, though she'd be just as happy with mugs and Nescafé. I wish I could tell her about the iceman but she'd misunderstand my fascination. We've been friends for half a century, but it wouldn't surprise me to hear it whispered uptown—*Mary Beth MacCallum's in love with a corpse.* Ellen is a bit of a gossip.

*

"Imagine. Advertising for a husband." What else can I say as she snaps the fold in the personals and snorts to herself? I should have hidden the paper too, under my bed, someplace she wouldn't see it.

"Husband! I don't think that's what they have in mind," she snorts again after a few minutes. (Our chit-chat often misses a beat, but I'm used to that.) I touch the brooch at my throat, then twist the handle of Ellen's teacup towards her. The tea is skinning over, after the pains I took to serve hers hot and milky, the way she likes it.

"I haven't time for smut like that," I say. It figures that Ellen finds obscenity comical; she has always been a little coarse.

"Oh, come on, Mary Beth. If I were fifty years younger I'd put an ad in myself." She hauls up the brassiere strap that's slithered down her bare arm, cutting into the droopy flesh, and I'm glad Oram isn't alive to hear this. A stupid man, Ellen's spouse, but entitled to more. I glare at her over the mauve roses on my cup, pursing my lips.

"You mustn't say things you don't mean, Ellen."

"No harm in a little bit of foolishness, Mary Beth."

"Fifty years ago you were a young bride."

"Forty-four."

"Oram was just back from overseas."

Ellen snatches a digestive biscuit from the silver tray.

"If you don't mind me saying, Mary Beth, you know precious little about married life." Before, she had the delicacy not to make such pronouncements, but now she watches me bristle.

"From what I saw of yours, I know all I need to." I toss aside the crocheted tea cosy to warm up her drink, and she looks askance at it, Phentex and lace like a doll's skirt—her Christmas gift to me.

"I don't know what you mean." She tucks the cosy over the pot. "But seriously, Mary Beth, there must be times you feel *cheated*."

"How can I regret what I never had?" My voice is brittle, and I feel weary. I want her to leave, though she'll likely stay the afternoon. The room suddenly feels stifling, the breeze off the harbour having shifted, leaving the air thick and languid. I feel my age, feel sluggish and out of patience with Ellen's nonsense. Yet she settles back on the sofa, fanning herself with the paper.

"Summer's early this year. Why, just last week there was still drift ice in the harbour," she prattles on. As if I hadn't seen it, hadn't spent every June of my eighty-five years in this place, watching the ocean.

"Yes. Yes." My eyes wander to the magazine at the bottom of the stack before us. If only we could have a real conversation. I worry my pink napkin into a wrinkled ball. The odd thing is that I depend on Ellen for the only companionship to be had in this town. Her mind was livelier, perhaps, when Oram was still alive and she needed someone of discretion to complain to. Not that her complaints weren't legitimate, with his drinking and womanizing—the latter being nasty rumour as far as I could see. Oram was no saint, to be sure, but Ellen knew that and willingly made her bed with him, set herself up to mend his socks.

"How about a fresh pot, Mary Beth?" she says, and before I can object she trots off to put the kettle on again. Next I hear her rustling through the bag of Peak Freans.

I suppose I've always seemed a good listener. Too good a listener to be much of a doer, Ellen had the gall to accuse me once. It was after Oram's wake; she was leaning on my arm as we left the funeral parlour. She was a bit hysterical, poor thing, and had knelt by the casket (closed, thank God) forgiving Oram's transgressions, listing the times he'd staggered in with rum on his breath or laid his hand on a woman's shoulder at a Legion dance. They were switching off all the lights in the parlour, gently shooing us out, the bereaved and their guests, darkness swallowing up the deceased and the living with the potted ferns. She was hating to leave Oram there alone with the other cadavers, I knew, so I excused her unkindness to me. I was distraught too at leaving Oram defenceless—though Ellen couldn't have known. All those years hearing about Oram's bad habits—the most intimate things, too. The way he wore his watch to bed every night and left scratches on her bosom. She had no idea how these confidences hurt me.

"Whatcha reading these days, Mary Beth?" she says again, the hot teapot wobbling on the tray. To please me she thumbs through the stack of *Digests*. To my dismay she snatches up the bottom one, which flips open to the iceman, the spine of the magazine split from my lingering over him.

"Lordy!" She gapes at the glossy pictures, the coppery, sinewed body laid out on a stainless steel table. *It's a laboratory, not a mortuary*, I want to explain, but her greedy eyes sap my strength. Her gaze is as blunt and rude as the salvagers' shovels, and I have to turn away when she studies the place where he was desecrated.

"Would you look at that?" she gasps in disgust. "Now, there's an argument for cremation! Even Hindu-style."

"Poor bugger!" she adds as I rise sharply, knocking the tea tray, trying to escape to the kitchen. Too late. "The smell must be something awful!" she mutters as I rinse my cup at the sink. Already she has begun to spoil him for me, making a lovely, perfect creature seem as defenceless and mortal as poor Oram.

*

Autumn, 1945. Oram is just back from Holland, has work lined up in the company offices—some sort of accounting work, listing the miners' tonnage. Whatever it is, I'm not interested. He has started calling me, trying to pick up threads left dangling before the war. I've had my pupils, haven't been *waiting* for him by any stretch, though let's just say no other fish have jumped. Ellen and I are at the Grey school together; she has grade four, I have grade five. We chat at recess, shivering on the steps, taking turns breaking up games of skipping and red rover and ringing her little brass handbell. Ellen wears gloves even on these gilded autumn mornings, sunlight rippling through the yellow elms that shade the schoolyard.

Oram bounds up the steps like a tardy student, to meet me after school. A Wednesday afternoon, the afternoon the company lets its clerks off early. As he opens the creaky double doors for me, Ellen appears from behind, her dull reddish hair unfurling from its pins. She removes her glove to pump Oram's outstretched hand, but I think nothing of this as she hurries ahead and Oram and I stroll down the cracked, dusty sidewalk to the co-op store. I have agreed to go for an ice-cream float.

"In France I never noticed the leaves falling," he says, watching Ellen's stocky calves wobbling ahead. The leaves above us are shirred with red and I laugh good-naturedly, clasping my lesson plans against the front of my cornflower-blue cardigan.

"Shall we have strawberry or vanilla?"

"Did you ever think of me while I was away?"

I pause, a long pocket of silence, because in truth I didn't.

"Now Oram, school kept me pretty well occupied." I swing through the finger-smudged glass door of the co-op, the dirty wooden floor groaning underfoot. We sit down at the soda fountain.

"I hoped maybe I meant more to you than that."

I let my strawberry drink go flat, pink scum like deflated candy floss around the middle of the fancy glass.

Oram slurps down the dregs of his, little traces of pink at the corners of his mouth. I'm sorry now I allowed him to meet me at school, and I wish I hadn't introduced him to Ellen—he looks so awkward and robust out of the ill-fitting uniform.

"I missed you, Mary Beth." The Purves girl behind the counter can hear every word, is probably making notes.

"So you've said."

"You haven't changed. . . ."

"Not much, no." How could I have, pinned to this town all this time? I'm starting to find his scrutiny quite repulsive, his watery blue eyes so hopeful, so steadfast, like an infant's.

"I didn't think you'd still be here."

The backs of my stockings feel glued to the swivelling stool, my tweed skirt itching through them. Drifting around the store are mothers of my pupils, buying spools of thread and sacks of flour, cards of bobby pins. From time to time they glance over to the soda fountain.

"I really must be off."

"I thought we might have supper."

"I have arithmetic to mark."

And that was the last time Oram and I spent alone together, because the next Saturday, when I was in the co-op purchasing yard goods, who should be sitting beside him at the counter but Ellen, her round bottom folding like bread dough over the stool? I could see it was more than a chance encounter by the way she dug her high heel into the footrail to pivot herself sideways, so Oram had to speak to the right side of her face. *Her better side, her more flattering profile,* she had confided one recess. She looked triumphantly over his shoulder at everyone coming in and out the door.

"Mary Beth!" she called when she saw me rooting for a nickel in my change purse, a length of grey suiting under my arm. Oram glanced around and smiled blandly, like a child caught pinching a penny liquorice.

"Can we treat you?" he asked half-heartedly as Ellen crossed her stubby legs, perching straight up on her stool.

"Your school wardrobe?" she cooed, mocking me with her fluttery eyes. Her green velvet peplum wasn't something she usually wore—certainly not to school. "Have a cup of tea before you go off to your sewing?"

"No. Thanks."

"Maybe another time." And they swivelled away from me, Oram spooning sugar into his cup.

After that I never saw them apart, except when Ellen was at school. She and I still chatted at recess, but there was little time for serious talk, what with breaking up fistfights and wiping the odd bloody nose. She continued to confide tips on home permanents and how to sew a kick pleat. We never discussed Oram—there wasn't much to say about him, really, except how he was getting on at the company.

A few months later they were married, in a big flowery affair at the United Church; I was invited along with half the town. Ellen looked lovely, if a little bulky, under her frothy gown. That set off the usual whisperings, but sometime after the wedding she had a miscarriage, and she and Oram never did have any children.

I can honestly say I was never jealous of Ellen—never felt malice or envy towards her; nothing more than impatience, the sort that bubbled up from time to time when she talked too much or said the wrong thing. Actually I felt indebted to Ellen for stealing Oram's attention, and in time I began accepting their invitations to supper. With the ham and scalloped potatoes Oram would offer us glasses of the sweet sherry he kept under the cupboard, but as long as I was there Ellen always declined. And Oram, being gentlemanly if not suave, never pressed us. As time went on and Ellen's chat at recess turned from perms to marital transgressions, we were all a little relieved when Oram started taking the bottle into the parlour after supper and polishing it off. After the rumours about him at the Legion, I rather dreaded what might come up at the table. Not because anything either of them might say would hurt me, but because I hated to feel like an interloper. More than once I'd heard it whispered in the co-op that I was the third wheel. Not that this offended me, you see, because I neither liked nor disliked Ellen and her husband. It was just that circumstances afforded us a certain camaraderie. It never occurred to me to be bitter that they had chosen one another over and above me, or that I was the one Ellen sought to burden with her miseries. Many a night, even after Oram's lungs got bad, the three of us sat together on their settee, watching the embers from a little blaze of shore coal, thinking up proverbs for games of charades. Even when the two of them weren't speaking, the three of us laughed over the possibilities—*straw that broke the camel's back, a stitch in time*. I never doubted their love for one another, even when Ellen came to school in a rage, saying she hoped Oram drank himself into the ground just so she could be free of him. I never did put much store in what Ellen said.

*

"Don't you ever wish you'd married?" she asked me one evening, a month or two before Oram's funeral. We were at the shore in my little Morris, the windows rolled up to keep warm, having our last cigarette before school started the next week. The sun was dull orange, sinking over the strait; the water was choppy with the kind of nor'easter that means fall's not far off.

"You know me. I'm glad I have no man to worry about." I instantly regretted it, certain she would take it as a slur. But for once she didn't.

"But haven't you been *lonesome*?" she said, as if I'd been robbed of a kettle of gold. Cheated.

"How can you say such a thing? I've had you—and Oram," I added reluctantly, sensing he'd given her some new cause for grief, hoping I wouldn't have to hear about it.

*

Oram's been gone five years now, and unless Ellen brings him up I rarely think of him. So I find it odd when he enters my dream the night after our little tea. He appears to me tilted up in his hospital bed, Ellen wringing her pudgy hands beside him, pale tears streaming down her cheeks. She's crying buckets with no sound coming out. His eyes are closed, roving from side to side under sallow, blue-veined lids, the sickly yellow flesh caving in on his corded neck, his deathly snore in and out through the mouth, bluish lips cracked and scabbed over with blackened blood. His orange-stained thumb and forefinger twittering and jolting up to his lips, like birds on a hot wire, a jagged, foolish motion like the twitches of a puppy dreaming. The tumour in his chest bulges through the starched white sheet.

"He wants a cigarette," I prod Ellen, who's beyond hearing. The nurses have told her he won't last till suppertime. She doesn't move, sits there like a mannequin in the Smart Shop window, not blinking, just allowing the rivers of tears to drip off her chin down the front of her blouse. A nurse comes in and tucks the live-wire hand under the stiff draw-sheet. The snores grow rougher, till I have to look away and study the black flecks in the speckled tiles. The hospital floor looks like polished granite.

When I glance up the linen is frozen, a snowy bed cradling Oram's withered body. The hand has stopped twitching, rests now under the folds, the mouth agape in a noiseless howl. His eyes, mercifully, are frozen shut. And though Ellen and I stare at him for hours before the nurse comes in to cover his face, it seems something miraculous is happening. His skin keeps its sallow tinge, not the purplish hue we are dreading, and gradually the features relax into a peaceful mask, an easy sleep, the limbs supple and dense again as in youth.

Oram's youth: his warm, heavy body crushing the sweet grass beneath the lilacs at MacIsaac's old place. We have wandered up the lane to the abandoned farmhouse, overrun with spruces and daisies: *nobody will find us here.* Oram drags me down into the nodding grass, the lilacs brown and drooping overhead. He leans over me, pressing himself against my thin, bony hips, pries my mouth open with his tongue. My mouth bruised and stupid, I say nothing as he fumbles with buttons, the side zipper of my skirt. The urgent swollen feeling down *there*, blood rising, bursting to meet the same instinct in his strange flesh. *Wanting him, wanting him so badly there is nothing else.* The sickly scent of the lilacs, the flies buzzing, all incidental to the secret, musky odour of our bodies, *the having to, having to. . . .*

"Will you wait for me," he pleads, breathlessly. He is so close to me.

How can I say anything but yes? *Yes, I will wait for you. I will do anything you say. If only I. . . .* But something makes me roll away from him and jump to my feet, picking bits of dead grass from my pale yellow blouse, twisted and crushed around my breasts, yarding my skirt back into place, the zipper nudging at my hip.

"I can't do this," I mutter, my eyes starting to smart. "I can't promise you anything either."

"It's not for ever." It strikes me that he thinks I'm distraught about him enlisting; how dare I correct him? There aren't words to explain why I can't give in to my desire or to his demand, so I'll leave it at that. I will myself to forget this happened, and choose instead to remember how he reached up then into the branches and snapped off some withered, grape-clustered blossoms and stuck them into my closed fists.

Ellen never knew, but maybe she sensed it. Yes, she must

have sensed something—otherwise why hang around me all these years, if not looking for confirmation? They say we all have a skeleton in our closet, that you can never really know a person. Not completely. But maybe Ellen has been trying to see me from the inside out, look through me like an X-ray or that newfangled ultrasound they used to chart Oram's cancer. And that's why she has kept so close all this time.

*

When I wake up I try to finish reading the article about the iceman, but somehow he has lost his appeal. He now appears rather distasteful, putrid as a well-waxed apple left too long in the cellar, glossy red skin but bruised to the core. He looks exposed and, in being uncovered, given up by the glacier, robbed of his quirky immortality. A corpse, after all, and left unburied for so long that a funeral would be a travesty. Mourned once, maybe, but outliving his mourners, lips drawn back over his top teeth in a half-grin. So what to do with him? The joke, after all, is on us, the survivors, and I think it's time to send him packing. No stopping now he's been thawed; better the glacier had kept its secret from our prying eyes. I can no longer study his shrivelled eyeballs; I can't stand to imagine what went on behind them before they left off staring into the snowfall.

I suppose I might have told Ellen about Oram and me if things had turned out differently. If Oram had not gotten sick but lived on to embarrass or shame her more deliberately. If there had been more between us, Ellen and me. If Oram had wanted to waltz with me at the Legion or tried to take my hand under the plywood table-top, if I had been one of those women he supposedly pursued. Oram a skirt chaser? I still don't believe it, though maybe I made him that way by refusing him under the lilacs. I confused him, showing both desire and denial, especially when it seemed—however fleetingly—that love might be worth the wait.

But I could never have loved him in return, in spite of wanting him. The body plays tricks on us, and to have given into mine that day would have challenged fate. No, I am not at all sorry for having lived out my life without Oram, or any man for that matter. My desire for solitude has always been deeper, and in the end the mind has it all over the flesh. That's nothing new. So there's no point in telling Ellen—why upset things now? Maybe, foolish me, she has known about it all along; perhaps my little secret is what brought her and Oram together.

I could weep now, shutting the *Digest* on the iceman's picture. I press the garbage pail open with my foot and shove the magazine down among the carrot peels and soggy teabags. To think I could have marvelled at such a thing. Ellen was right; he is a good argument for cremation, for dying in hospital. I go to the sink and rinse out the teapot, letting the water run awhile before I fill up the kettle.

Meet Me at the Ex

Sure—I stood up Lauchie Abbott that sticky night and missed a free night's fun at the Exhibition. So much dull excitement, the happy tortured shrieks of girls on the Ferris wheel like people being tickled to death, and side-stepping candy floss and cigarette butts ground into the dirt. I would have liked it: an evening's forgetting we were in Blackett, coal-town dinginess tripped and tilted into the soft pitch sky aswirl with lights and off-key calliope. Blackett transformed. But admission price would have been Lauchie's sweaty kisses or, worse, some desperate groping behind the Wheel of Fortune booth. What if he had won me a green plush panda? I would have been sunk for sure then, by the time the tattooed, black-toothed roustabouts collapsed the Ferris wheel and the stuttering carousel and moved someplace else, Glace Bay or New Waterford. Nothing left but a sooty patch of bare ground, no sign at all that the midway had come and gone, and everything as bleak and haphazard as before.

Blackett was the type of town where nobody finished what they started: houses half-painted till the shingles rotted, one wall mud-brown, the rest left silvery grey. Bootleg pits out in the fields behind the town hall and the liquor store, sunk during an early snow, then abandoned if the cash came through to buy company coal. At seventeen Lauchie Abbott was just like Blackett, finished in a half-baked way, stunted and spent before it ever chanced to prosper.

But this wasn't my impression the day my brother Arch brought him over to tinker with the Ford. I was at the kitchen table peeling potatoes when they came in for a drink of water, trailing engine grease on Ma's fresh-scrubbed linoleum, a whiff of tobacco from their sweat-stained shirts. Arch had quit grade twelve a month before graduation to pump gas at MacKiggan's garage and save up for the car. I suppose that's where he met Lauchie, who like Arch would have been a few years ahead of me if he had stayed at school. He was from Pit Street, down by the washplant, and Ma sniffed when he and Arch came in the house and left grease marks all over the big enamel sink. They rumbled past me as if I weren't there—Arch's baby sister, the youngest of nine kids, the only girl in the family. I felt like sticking my head in the big tin pot of potatoes; I was fourteen and scared I looked like Ma, half-moons of sweat under the arms of my navy jumper and my hair all stringy from the steamy kitchen.

Ma didn't speak or smile. When Lauchie muttered, "Hello, Mrs. Gillis," slicking back his dull black hair with the heel of his hand, Ma turned sharply and went to rummage for something in the pantry.

"When's supper, Ma?" Arch said, wiping his hands on the dishtowel drying on the oven door, tossing it to Lauchie when he was done. I peeked up from the heap of peelings and found Lauchie watching me, not smiling but observing me with small, birdlike eyes full of what I took to be contempt. I looked down quickly and started on another potato.

"That's enough," Ma said pointedly. "It's just you and Arch and me for supper, you know. We're not feeding an army." Her rudeness shocked me and I remember glaring at her, mortified. It was not her way, or the way of anyone who lived in Blackett, to appear stingy, especially with food. But Lauchie seemed not to notice and followed Arch outside, and whistled as they finished fiddling under the hood. I listened to his tinny laugh, his cheerful cough as he smoked cigarettes from the pack tucked up inside his short sleeve, while the smell of grease and engine oil came through Ma's white lace curtains and mingled with that of potatoes boiling on the big white range. It was an unusually sultry afternoon in late June, and Lauchie wore a greyish undershirt while Arch had on a regular shirt with the sleeves rolled up. I could tell Ma was insulted by the way she banged the pot lids.

"Families go to the dogs once the mother's gone," she finally sighed, as if that were the kindest excuse she could muster for Lauchie Abbott—and for her own lack of charity, as if having no mother made him more culpable. I figured she blamed him for Arch's lack of ambition, for his buying a car that refused to run after the one trip from MacKiggan's to our yard. And with dread I understood that her unkindness was meant to protect me; I was too young for boyfriends, she said. The tilt of her eyebrow implied that I (if not Arch) should stay clear of people like the Abbotts, who ran a grubby little dairy opposite the pithead with cigarettes and a few tinned goods behind the counter. I had never been inside, but I imagined it was the kind of store where tins of peas and corned beef left white rings on the shelves if anyone bought them.

Like the rest of the town, I knew all about the Abbotts. Lauchie's mother was dead and his father ran the store, smoking cigarettes all day in a rickety wheelchair behind the cashbox, his legs lost in a cave-in at the pit. He kept shop in order to feed eight children, of whom Lauchie was the oldest.

My father—a foreman above ground—had died when I was nine, killed slowly (the doctor said) by years of breathing coal dust. I suppose this might have given Lauchie and me something in common, but our house was on the other side of town, on a street shaded by chestnuts, almost out of sight of the mine. The only reminder of it was the screech and grind of coal cars wheeling and coupling in the railyard behind our garden. And especially after Pa got cancer—a slow tortured death rather than the sharp release from life caused by a gas explosion or roof collapse—Ma closed her eyes to the pit and aimed to wash her hands of coal for ever. She still depended on it to keep us warm and cook our meals, of course, but after Pa's death she tried to forget the mine existed. She may have even yearned to leave Blackett, but that possibility didn't exist, and she was too practical to daydream about it. It was too late for her to entertain such fantasies for herself, but she passed them on to me as subtly as the brown sugar she sprinkled on porridge, which melted in so fast you always craved more.

But getting away from Blackett wasn't just a dream of Ma's. From the time you entered the Grey school, it was passed on with the alphabet and times-tables that anyone worth their salt would have to leave if they hoped to make anything of themselves. Yet by the time I started high school half the boys in my class had quit to follow their dads underground, tunnelling under the floor of the sea, learning the sounds of the mine and surviving on intuition until either their luck ran out or they lived to retire.

By the time Pa died there was just Arch and me home; all the others, all seven of Ma's other sons, had already taken off for the west, places like Grande Cache and Prince Rupert, mining towns where the pay was better and they had safety standards. Or so my brothers told Ma in their thin, infrequent letters, which she kept bound together with rubber bands inside the cardboard jewellery box on her dresser. They were seeking "a better life" was how she excused them, and as far as we knew this was what they found in these places, dots on a map, too far away for us to visit. At fourteen I had no wish to see the towns where my brothers had settled, met and married local girls and had children; why travel thousands of miles to see more of what I sensed I should try to escape? And Arch refused to go, though his prospects by then seemed more limited than mine. We never talked about it—he and I had little to say to one another—but I think he shared my feeling that if you went to one of these places you would simply vanish into the deeps, or be swallowed up among strangers in a vague and unfamiliar place. At least in Blackett the dangers were known and easily spotted.

And I, being Ma's only daughter, wanted nothing to do with mines or miners or anything that reminded me of them, the constant smell of coal tar, the blackened ground like a burnt offering. I had plans for myself, to stroll down paved streets and to browse past plate-glass storefronts, not the dusty window of the co-op store, full of enamelled pots and rubber boots and bags of potatoes.

"Best quality on the island," Ma always huffed when I accompanied her on her weekly shopping trips uptown, which after Pa's funeral were more for looking than buying. I longed to take the train to Halifax, to finger store-made dresses and real underwear, not the kind Ma made for me from sugar bags. Some girls at school had sisters who moved there and got married, and I wondered (with as much awe as the others) how it would be to boil water on an electric stove instead of a coal-burning Enterprise, to live a clean, breezy life unsmudged by coal dust. (One of these sisters, it was rumoured, got a fox stole from her husband one Christmas, and vowed to return to Blackett just to show it off. Whether she ever did, I don't know.)

But these were the last things on my mind that day Arch brought Lauchie over to work on his car. You see, Lauchie Abbott carried his family's aura of tragedy—as well as miracle, the miracle of survival—though it was diminished somehow when you saw the store and the dingy, cracked windows of their upstairs flat. There, people said, the kids kept the father in bed so his wheelchair could be left in place down in the store.

Looking back, maybe I was attracted to people stricken with bad luck, to those clearly worse off than me; I suppose in a bleak way they seemed glamorous. But that day Lauchie Abbott was tinkering with the car, now so far in the past, I simply felt surprised that he could crack jokes, peering with Arch under the hood, as if nothing mattered but spark plugs and fan belts. It made me wonder about him, if only because his home life was such common property in Blackett, dredged up like those bootleg pits in the fields. Besides that there was no reason to take an interest in him, in fact, after seeing him in our kitchen, I could hardly recall what he looked like. Odd in a town that size, where I'd no doubt seen him around.

So I was stunned the next morning when Arch said, "Lauchie wants to know if you'll go for a walk wit' him sometime." It caught me off guard, and I racked my brain trying to conjure up some picture of him from the day before— something to thrill over, to look forward to with a tingle of anticipation. I had little to go on, having stared at the potatoes most of the time.

"Oh?" I said coolly, hoping Arch couldn't see the effect of such sudden, fortuitous flattery. I glanced over at Ma washing up, praying she wouldn't see the flush in my cheeks, but she went on scouring the porridge pot. Though Arch and I didn't talk much, we both knew enough to keep certain things from her, and that was the last I heard of Lauchie's proposition.

All that morning, the last day of grade nine, I squirmed in my seat—not because, like the others, I was desperate to know if I'd graded, but because I kept working on that picture of Lauchie Abbott's face, feature by feature. By noon dismissal I had composed a movie-star image of glowing skin, a gleaming black duck-tail, deep dark eyes. *Elvis eyes, bedroom eyes*, a term I heard in the schoolyard and understood well enough not to repeat it around Ma. And when Arch came in from the garage and stood washing his hands at the sink, I whispered, "Yes. You can tell Lauchie I'll go for a walk."

I was never really invited on a date; Lauchie simply showed up a few days later, after lunch, when Arch was heading back to the garage. Ma was ironing sheets and didn't notice me slip outside with them.

"Nice day," Lauchie said stiffly as the three of us trotted uptown, me between them, running to keep up.

"Too muggy, feels like thunder," Arch grumbled, not much in the mood for work.

"Naw," said Lauchie, "it can't rain openin' night at the

Ex." My brother grunted, then reddened slightly. "Wouldn' wanna miss that, Arch, wudja? 'Specially not stuck in some back seat." The two of them whooped at that and Arch got even redder. I ignored it, trying my best to keep up with them until we reached MacKiggan's and Arch sauntered over to the pumps.

"Take 'er easy, b'y," he yelled, not looking at me, and for the first time I was able to steal a good look at Lauchie. So much for Elvis, I decided, dismayed that I could have fabricated so much from so little. God knows how I had overlooked his ugliness. It would have been understandable, forgivable even, if he'd been pale and easily forgotten. But all I saw was greasy hair and blackheads, a beakish nose that curled over his big yellow teeth. I wanted to cry, I wanted to say there had been some mistake . . . but I pitied him and I tried, I really did, not to dwell on what I saw or show my disgust.

He edged closer, as if to take Arch's place, and I couldn't help noticing his odour, of sweat and urine-stained under-clothes and oily, unwashed skin. I made myself remember his dead mother and his maimed father.

"So," he said, "Arch's tol' me all 'boutcha."

"Oh?" I was squirming like a beetle under a magnifying glass as we headed towards the busiest stretch of Main Street. I tugged at his grimy sleeve, desperate for some escape. "The shore, let's go down by the cliff." It was hardly a romantic suggestion—the cliff was an eroded slag heap overlooking the tar pond and some ruined coke ovens. Nobody I knew came from that end of Atlantic Street, lined by Insul-brick shacks and the shells of wrecked cars, an area shunned by Ma and our neighbours.

"The clift? Yeah, sure," he agreed obligingly, a confused gleam in his small eyes. I could tell he was hoping my urge for seclusion was really some kind of invitation.

"It's a good place to talk," I fumbled, hoping that would throw him off and make the cliff seem less significant, less like a secret I wished to share. It never occurred to me that leading him off the beaten path might seem like an offer of something furtive, illicit.

Lauchie marched along beside me to Atlantic Street, where the people and cars began to thin out, picket fences and gardens giving way to weeds and alders and a sulphurous-smelling bog. Then he grinned and made a grab for my hand. I snatched it away, making fists in the pockets of my sundress, a pale flowered cotton which Ma had finished the night before. I imagined Lauchie Abbott's grubby fingers on it and started walking faster; I had worn flimsy white sandals, the only shoes I had to match my dress, and as we began scaling the slag hill, its moonscape surface of bubbled grey chunks crumbling underfoot, one of the straps let go. Lauchie bent to fix it but I hobbled away, cringing at the thought of him touching my foot. All the time he kept talking—though I no longer remember what about—as if his good-natured chit-chat would win me over.

"Yer not a bit like Arch," he said after we descended the other side of the slag heap and started past the shaft below Pit Street. It was the first real comment about family either of us had made and though his remark hardly seemed a prelude to unwanted confidences, I felt myself stiffen up.

"Arch is just one o' da guys. But you, now, you seem right diff'rent." It was as easily an insult as a compliment.

"I guess so," I muttered, waiting for him to start in about his family. If I said I already knew, would he spare me the details?

"I have sisters," he began. "But they ain't like you."

I limped along faster, my sandal slapping the dirt. If he told me about his mother, his crippled father, about his brothers and sisters having to carry the old man to the toilet, I would *have* to hold his hand, to slow down and smile at him. Girls were supposed to be sympathetic, to offer themselves as a comfort; I knew because I had seen Ma do it, and not just after Pa got sick.

Then Lauchie stopped and pulled me close, his black nails

digging into my arm. "My sisters are sluts," he announced, watching my face. When he saw my relief he looked bewildered, and then he sneered, "My ol' lady was a slut too." I pictured my own mother in her faded aprons and my jaw dropped. He stopped talking after that.

As we turned up Pit Street the faded "Drink Coca-Cola" sign outside Abbott's dairy seemed to beckon from across the potholed road. I pretended not to see it, but as we approached Lauchie grabbed my hand, lacing his grimy fingers through mine. I tried not to notice how damp and fleshy they felt, like spoiled sausages, and stared at the copper roof of the post office uptown, expecting him to steer me across to that weedy, litter-strewn side of the street and up the lopsided steps into the store. I started rehearsing what I might say to the man behind the counter. But miraculously Lauchie kept walking, smiling as smugly as a man out for a stroll with his bride. Glancing sideways, I was struck by the contentment on his face; I was so relieved at passing the store that I forgot to anticipate the hazard ahead, a hazard worse than the squalor of Abbott's dairy. And as I marched hand in hand with Lauchie towards the cenotaph—him grinning like he had struck gold or won a fight—I didn't notice the teenagers hanging around the monument until it was too late to shake off his grip and bolt away. Had I seen them ahead, I would have wasted no time on excuses and jumped the nearest fence into a yard or vegetable patch—anything to avoid them.

But they saw me first, or I should say they saw us first, Grace Gillis and Lauchie Abbott walking uptown *holding hands*. Lauchie looking like the cat that caught the canary. There were some girls from my class and a bunch of boys from grade eleven, lolling around the monument the way they always do on summer afternoons. As if they had nothing better to do. There was Peggy Hinch and Bertie Lamb and some others I recognized, and when we got closer they started hooting. As we passed, the giggling burst into belly-laughter so loose and carefree they might have been rolling on the ground like animals. I wanted to die right there on the dusty sidewalk.

"Wudja lookit the lovebirds!" they cackled like squawking gulls, and began to sing, *Gracie and Lauchie up a tree, K-I-S-S-I-N-G! First comes love, then comes marriage. Then comes Gracie with a baby—* And then somebody hissed, "She must be some friggin' desperate."

I was red as a brick, but I held my head high and tried to imagine myself miles away, in Halifax perhaps, the boy beside me just some grubby stranger, a panhandler or vagrant following me down the street.

Lauchie stuck out his chin to hide his overbite until his yellow teeth left pale dents in his bottom lip, all the while keeping up his foolish, sly grin. He didn't glance back or say a word, just kept walking with my hand in a death-grip until we reached the top of the hill, where Pit Street met the main drag. Then he smiled and said, "Wanna come to the Ex t'night? Meet me at seven by the gates. Seven o'clock," he repeated, giving me no chance to refuse. And I agreed, knowing I wouldn't be there but lacking the heart or the wherewithal to say no.

I tottered down Main Street as fast as possible on my broken sandal, and when I got home I ran a bath, a cold shallow bath in our damp little bathroom with its turquoise-stained sink and dank odour of toothpaste and town water. After supper I told Ma I had cramps and went straight to bed, burrowing under the flour-bag quilt, though even with the dark-green blind drawn it was still quite light, and warm, too, a perfect summer evening. I imagined other girls in full, twirling skirts and bright lipstick, their high-pitched chatter and happy screams rising with the scent of candy floss and tobacco into the dusky air over the fairgrounds. The sharp bite of a candy apple under its brittle, sweet coating, the hard red glaze cracking and melting all at once. And Lauchie hanging around the turnstile like a drooling retriever, asking the man taking tickets if he was sure of the time.

All evening I lay under the quilt, hand-stitched of worn scraps of cloth left over from clothes of mine and Ma's and even Granny's. I made myself remember each dress, each blouse, as I listened for the phone to ring or him banging on the kitchen door asking Ma where the hell I was, blaming her for my not showing up. Once I thought I heard her downstairs explaining, her voice muffled by the radio, but when nothing happened I realized it was just a neighbour. You see, I expected some punishment, I almost wished for it so I could apologize and put the whole thing behind me. I wanted to be punished because for the first time I felt I had done something really bad, something cruel. Not merely deceitful, like fibbing to Ma about my marks or putting on lipstick behind her back—but nasty, because I had snubbed someone who, in spite of himself, deserved better. It had nothing to do with his dead mother or his crippled father—it had to do with how he had walked past the kids at the cenotaph as though they didn't exist.

But no punishment came. Around midnight I heard Arch stagger in, and before he stumped to his room he stuck his head in and laughed, "I hear ya stood up poor ol' Lauchie, eh? I seen him uptown t'night and all he could say was, 'She stood me up, didn't she, Arch? *She stood me up*,' like he was waitin' for me to apologize or somethin'. I told him, *it ain't my business what she does*, but he kept after me, sayin', 'She stood me up, she stood me up,' like he wanted me to fight over it. 'Ha!' I said. 'You think I give a *goddamn* about it?'" Arch laughed again, that cruel, ragged laugh he had when he'd been drinking, a laugh that made him sound five times his age.

After that night Lauchie stopped coming around and nobody mentioned his name again. Mysteriously the summer holidays seemed to wipe out the town's memories of my walk with him, my classmates moving on to more spectacular bits of gossip. And although a few more years passed before I finished high school and was able to leave Blackett, our paths never crossed there again. I have to admit I forgot all about him, my guilt over standing him up fading with time and other priorities, like keeping up my grades for secretarial school in Halifax and, later, looking nice for John Alec MacNeil. I graduated from grade twelve and that pleased Ma no end. But my marks didn't buy my train ticket to Halifax—it was John Alec who got me out of Blackett. He took me to the city, where we got married by a justice of the peace in a room full of strangers, a place full of paved streets and plans, my *big* plans.

I did see Lauchie Abbott once more, though—in a bar in Halifax a few months after my wedding. Things were not so good between John Alec and me; we were quarrelling a lot, fighting like cats and dogs, actually. This one night we left the apartment "to talk" and, as we sat glumly in a corner of the Ladies' Beverage Room watching the waiter plunk down dripping trays of draft, I heard someone call to me.

"Hello, Grace," he said from the next table, and it was so gloomy I had to squint to see who it was. It wasn't a voice I recognized and I knew few people in Halifax, just some acquaintances from our apartment house. At first I didn't recognize him at all—his hair was shorter and he seemed thinner, less doughy, and his acne was gone.

"How've you been?" he asked curtly, as John Alec gave him the evil eye and blew smoke rings in his direction. "You look well," he sneered, and I half expected him to curse at me, even after all this time.

"I'm not bad," I said, as he turned away to light a smoke for the woman beside him. Perhaps it sounded like a plea, for he left me alone after that. We might have sat there all night without shooting each other another glance. But I felt my penance was done, small as it was; whether it was accepted or not I would never know. I waited for John Alec to down his beer, then pulled him away, dragged him up the filthy tiled steps to the street. I waited for him to give me a going-over about Lauchie but for once he said nothing. The only thing that struck me was the sweetish, diesel-laced air of an uncommonly still June night.

The Game of Love

It took me all afternoon to get ready for the dance, pressing my blue dirndl skirt till the gathers were just *so*. Washing and setting my hair, a million spit-curls around my face—a *gigantic* waste of time, seeing how it rained later. But worth it. Worth every minute, even with Ma fussing and sighing around me about floors to be scrubbed, socks to be darned. She just didn't want me going to a Catholic dance, that's all. As if the Knights of Columbus were some kind of crusaders just waiting to carry off nice Protestant girls like me. Never mind there wasn't a soul in Blackett I'd have *wanted* to carry me away. Or so I let on.

"Watch yerself," she said, grabbing the iron from me to do around the zipper. "If you're not careful you'll melt it."

I stood back and let her finish off my skirt, determined not to argue. But no way was I backing down; this was the first Saturday night after graduation, and my whole class was going, Catholic or not. I'd never been inside the Knights' hall—the name alone was enough to attract me. I pictured grown men dressed up in armour, ready to joust for the honour of daughters and nieces. Honour being something we felt more and more burdened with, like a strawberry birthmark or heavy thighs.

Ardith MacEachern, who was Catholic, assured me her father and uncles were like anybody else's.

"Don't be silly," I sighed into the phone. "*Of course* I know that." All the same, it gave me a thrill saying, "See ya at the

K.O.C., eight o'clock, out front." Though from the street the place looked ordinary enough, a tall, white-shingled building with a pitched roof, next to the garage.

"I'll get Arch to come for ya at eleven," Ma said, hobbling after me with her mouth full of pins. "Yer hem's draggin' a little in back."

"God no, Ma. I'll get a drive with one of the girls," I said, standing still so she could fix it. The thought of my brother lumbering through the couples, peering over their heads for me, made the skin on my shoulders crawl.

"Don't worry—I'll be home soon as it's over."

"Mind you don't get into any strange cars. And stay up by the stage, away from the back. Them Catholics like their liquor, I've heard."

In the bathroom I let her take out the bobby pins, the rough pressure of her fingers on my scalp while I watched in the mirror, sucking in my cheeks. The wavy glass made my face look longer, my grey eyes deeper set.

"That's enough." Ma gave me a little whack on the neck. "No foolishness, now, you hear me? Them people and their drinkin'—ya don't want no one takin' advantage—"

"Ma!"

"You know what I mean." Then she fished around in her apron, pulled out her round silver locket. A wisp of pale yellow baby hair inside—mine. She looped it over my collar, then went out into the hall, yanking the bathroom door shut behind her.

"Have a good time," I heard her call from the landing.

*

John Alec MacNeil was one of the fellows taking tickets, sitting on a stool in the narrow doorway, the light from the overhead bulb casting a reddish gleam on his dark hair. He was thin as a ladder, knees like saw-blades in his tight black pants, one pointy-toed boot tapping the floor in time to the music behind

—75—

him. I stared at his boots as I handed him my ticket, which he ripped in half, slapped into my damp palm. Behind him the band was warming up: the high-pitched twang of an electric guitar, the dull thrum of a bass. Fingering Ma's locket, I followed the other girls to one side of the hall, in darkness but for a red light over the stage. Hulking boys ranged along some benches opposite us, elbows on their knees, smoking cigarettes and guzzling pop. The girls pretended not to watch them pull bottles from their pockets to top up their Cokes. Twittering nervously, they stared at the band warming up, their eyes veering off every now and then to the boys. I huddled close to Ardith and Cheryl-Lynn Boucher, nodding as they whispered about who was with whom, all the time aware of the fellow taking tickets, listening for his low voice in between bits of songs.

I'd seen John Alec before, of course, afternoons Ardith, Cheryl-Lynn and I sat on the library steps watching the cars creep up and down Main Street. He was the fellow with the maroon Pontiac that burbled when he slowed for the intersection—the only traffic lights in the entire town. One time he'd glanced sideways at us, a smirk of a smile on his face, before he stepped on it and screeched away.

"Did you see that?" Ardith yelped, as Cheryl-Lynn fished up under her skirt to straighten her garter-belt.

"Huh?" she said, rolling a wad of gum on the tip of her tongue. Cheryl-Lynn could look so bovine at times. "Oh. *Him*," she sighed and resumed her chewing.

"He's got the hots for us, I can tell," Ardith shrieked, nudging the toe of her white boot into Cheryl-Lynn's rear.

"Shhhh!" I said, as two ladies in shapeless dresses and white cardigans strolled towards us, clutching their purses—friends of Ma's from the ladies' auxiliary. They smiled vaguely at me and kept going, heading for the Smart Shop. I stood up, dusting off the seat of my pedal-pushers.

"Oh," Cheryl-Lynn repeated. "Didn't he used to go out with that MacDonald one?"

"Russian hands!" Ardith gasped in a burst of laughter.

"Roman fingers!" giggled Cheryl-Lynn.

"Skin dog!" the two of them howled, rolling their eyes.

"Would you stop!" I hooted, collapsing in giggles on the bottom step, just missing a blob of spittle.

"*Oh shit*," Ardith said then, recovering in time to see Waynie MacLellan—one of the boys from our graduating class—shuffling along the sidewalk. The doctor's son, Waynie was a large boy with his hair combed back in thin strings that showed his scalp.

"Girls!" he shouted, coming closer and hovering over us on the steps. "How 'bout a ride in my old man's Buick? I know if I asked him he'd gimme the keys—"

He gazed down at Ardith's fluffy red hair, and at the pink triangle of skin at the top of her shell.

"Later, Waynie, later," she said, the three of us falling into one another laughing.

"Pretty bad," Waynie sneered, kicking at a crack in the cement. "Three girls with nothin' better to do than hang out on the library steps all day."

Ardith sniffed, her chin in her hands. Cheryl-Lynn craned behind her, peering down the street at the war monument, that other spot where teenagers gathered, the one we felt was a bit common. ("Them girls that hang out there are just out for *one thing*," Ardith liked reminding us.) No matter what a girl was after, the pickings were slim in Blackett. The way I saw it, I was just biding my time anyway. *You've got your whole life ahead of you*, Ma was always saying. I figured I'd get on at the Royal Bank for a while, stay there long enough to save up for business school in Halifax. Ardith had similar plans, but not my marks.

"Let's get *the hell* out of here," she said then, jumping up and slithering past Waynie's bulging stomach. He stepped back and the three of us staggered past, still giggling like loons.

We stopped in front of the Five-and-Ten.

"He's got his eye on you, Gracie!" Ardith blurted, tilting her face this way and that in the dingy window, examining a pimple.

"Thanks a lot!"

"Not Waynie, for Chrissake!" She dug her elbow into Cheryl-Lynn's side.

I made my face go blank, though under the pink blusher my cheeks were burning.

"Who, then?"

"You *knows* who she means, Grace. Don't give us that bullshit, girl!" Cheryl-Lynn said, collapsing against Ardith in yet another fit of giggles. I thought the two of them would wet their pants.

"No way!" I said, but they were too busy rolling their eyes and rubbing their fingers, like Boy Scouts rubbing sticks together to start a fire. A woman with a baby in her arms came out of the store, scowling at us as she tried to get past.

"Come on," Ardith said, finally straightening up. "I want some new nailpolish to match that lipstick I just got."

"Nah—"

"Suit yerself then," she sighed, Cheryl-Lynn following her inside. Through the dirty glass I could see them browsing in the narrow aisles, the reflection of cars sliding past. A steady stream of cars, most of them rusty and loud, but no maroon Pontiacs. I stood sideways, fluffing my hair and holding in my stomach.

"Who ya watchin' for?" Cheryl-Lynn winked when they came back outside, turning their wrists to compare the streaks of orange and pink painted there.

"Grace wouldn't look twice at no one in this town," said Ardith, blowing at some orange varnish on her pinkie.

"What's the matter wit' you, eh?" Cheryl-Lynn was watching me with her mascaraed eyes—raccoon eyes—her gum on the tip of her tongue.

"Who'd ya say he used to go with?" I asked, to make up for not going in the store. And the two of them fell on me, digging their elbows into my ribs, their breath warm and minty in my face.

"He's some cute," Cheryl-Lynn mooned. "Man, what I'd give to get behind *his* wheel!"

*

The band finally finished warming up. The guitar player and drummer were fellows from town, though they looked more exotic on stage, in Beatle haircuts and boots, than packing groceries or delivering coal. The red light over the stage started flashing on and off as they struck up their first number, "The Game of Love".

Ardith and Cheryl-Lynn sat mesmerized on wooden stacking chairs, mouthing the lyrics. They started, as if being shaken awake, when Waynie MacLellan and another fellow squeezed through the crowd and asked them to dance.

Bass notes humming in my throat, I sat there watching Waynie drape himself over Ardith's skinny shoulders, the other fellow kneading Cheryl-Lynn's upper arm like dough, his left hand sliding from her waist, drifting dangerously lower.

I got up and went to the washroom. When I came back they'd disappeared, and our seats had been taken by some older girls who sat in brooding silence, scanning the dance floor like crows. The music's tempo began to pick up, the drumbeat lagging slightly behind the chords of "Hang On Sloopy". The group of girls got up and started twisting, and then I spotted Ardith and Cheryl-Lynn near the door, talking to Waynie and someone else—John Alec. Ardith was hanging back a little, looking at her shoes and twisting the string of plastic beads around her neck.

"Grace!" she hissed, waving at me to come over, and I noticed the brown bag in Waynie's hand, the screw-top of a bottle sticking out. Ardith snatched the bottle and took a drink, pursing her lips the way old people take cough syrup, her eyes fastened on John Alec standing quietly with his thumbs hooked in his front pockets. He took the bag from her and shrugged, glancing at me.

Up close he looked about my age, or no more than a couple of years older, and not much taller. Waynie loomed over him like a tall, rather greasy-looking baby.

"Does yer friend want a drink?" John Alec grinned at Ardith and Cheryl-Lynn and I saw the girls nudging each other as he edged closer to me, his hand at my elbow.

Russian hands, Roman fingers. I prayed for once they'd keep their mouths shut.

"So what are we waitin' for?" said Waynie, and the bunch of us filed outside to the parking lot, the music echoing off the empty cars. It had started to spit rain and I followed, shivering, as the others piled into John Alec's car, the colour of prunes in the dim light from the hall.

Ardith and Cheryl-Lynn got into the back seat with Waynie as John Alec reached across the front to shove open the passenger door. I slid in, smoothing my skirt over my knees and folding my hands in my lap.

John Alec lit a cigarette and blew smoke rings at the windshield, flicking the wipers on every couple of minutes. Nobody said a word, the only sounds the slosh and swallowing of liquor from the back seat. A bald man came out of the hall and waved a flashlight over the cars in the lot, and a burst of nervous giggles erupted behind me. John Alec let the car idle, kept playing with the wipers.

"Could we *go* someplace?" Ardith said after a while, and John Alec put the car in gear and backed out onto the street, the cigarette dangling from his bottom lip. It was raining now, and the wipers beat monotonously as Ardith, Waynie and Cheryl-Lynn kept passing the bottle.

"Gimme that!" Waynie finally roared, grabbing the bottle and propping it between his knees. "Man, these girls are like fish," he said, and John Alec glanced across at me, a smile curling his lip. He had a faint growth of beard that made him look gaunt in the watery play of the streetlights.

"Someplace out of town!" Ardith giggled, wrestling the bottle away from Waynie. John Alec watched in the rearview, then looked at me and grinned.

"Wherever you want," he said, butting out his cigarette, his eyes on the shiny pavement.

We soon left Blackett behind, its lights rippling behind the dark heads in the back seat. I tried to concentrate on the road ahead, pretending to look at familiar spots along the way, the side of a barn, a toppled whirligig, as if I'd never seen them before. When it started to quiet down behind me, I glanced back at Ardith craning towards her window, Waynie's hand on her thigh. Cheryl-Lynn leaned the other way, sipping quietly from the bottle.

"Don't drink it all or nothin'," John Alec said over his shoulder, hugging the wheel. Somebody stifled a burp. He slowed down then, and pulled off the pavement to the low dirt road along the pond, and drove in silence till we reached the road to the beach.

"I feel sick," Ardith mumbled, and John Alec stopped and yanked her out by the arm. She stumbled around in the wet bushes; I squeezed my ears to shut out the sound of retching.

"Ya can dress 'em up but ya can't take 'em out," Waynie muttered stupidly. John Alec shook his head and lit another smoke, tossing the open pack on the seat beside me.

"Help yerself," he said, tugging up the collar of his windbreaker and raising his eyebrows at Waynie in the rearview. I reached over and took a cigarette, wondering how badly the smell would cling to my hair.

"What time is it?" I said.

"Aw, relax. The night's just young yet," Waynie crowed, winding down the window to check on Ardith. She staggered over and climbed in, moaning softly.

John Alec reached under the seat and pulled out a bottle of port. He unscrewed the top, took a long drink, then nudged it at me.

"I think they've had enough back there, don'tchu?"

Ardith leaned on Waynie's shoulder with her eyes clamped shut, breathing slowly. Snoring lightly, Cheryl-Lynn sat slumped against his other shoulder. I tried to tune out the smell of vomit.

"Jesus Christ. You watch yerself now." John Alec watched me take a sip of the thick sweet wine and blot my mouth carefully on the back of my wrist. "This yer first time or what?"

"No," I lied. Gripping the bottle in both hands, I took another, longer drink, trying not to gag. From the corner of my eye I could see Waynie's hand working its way up Cheryl-Lynn's short sleeve.

"I seen you before, I think," said John Alec. "You're a Gillis, right? Seen you the other day by the library." He was looking at me now, his eyes soft in the rainy darkness. He leaned his head back and seemed to be listening to the sound of gentle breathing in the back seat, the rain pelting the car roof.

I felt the warmth of the port in my ears, the soft rubbery feeling spreading to my limbs. John Alec turned slightly, his right foot braced against the driveshaft.

"Take 'er easy, Grace—last thing I need's another one fallin' asleep on me." He picked up the bottle and took another drink before thrusting it under the seat again. Behind us I heard Waynie cough, the rustle of his hand being shoved away.

"How old are ya, anyway?" John Alec asked, eyeing my top button, then glancing quickly away. He started drumming on the steering wheel with his fingers. I stole a good look at the side of his face, the smooth hollow in his cheek, the sharp outline of his nose.

"Seventeen," I said, my heart sinking as he started the car. "I think I saw you on Main Street the other day. I mean, it might have been you. You were driving—"

"Yer older'n I thought," he said, leaning his head out the window to back up. "You got a face could stop a clock, ya know that?"

"Oh God," I said, gnawing my lip to quell the happiness starting to swell inside me. "Guys don't say things like that."

"Naw? Well. *You do.* I'm not shittin' ya neither."

I breathed in deeply, ignoring the queasiness in my

stomach. I waited for more—for him to pull over or take my hand. Anything. But he kept his foot on the gas, his fingers tapping out a slow rhythm on the wheel. I bumped and jolted along in silence, aware now of my breasts jiggling under my blouse, my bra digging into my back and the sloshy feeling under my waistband.

When we got back to the paved road he lit another cigarette and started fumbling with the radio. *She Loves You* crackled through the darkness, the wipers going like the metronome at the glee club. And then another song came on, *Because I used to love her, but it's all over now,* John Alec humming along until the crackling got so bad he had to switch it off. I leaned my head back, let my hand fall on the seat between us. As we drove into town he moved his hand towards mine and gave it a squeeze, the cigarette clenched in his teeth, his eyes on the car ahead of us.

He seemed to know where I lived, veering onto the gravel in front of our place. A light was on upstairs—a good sign. At least Ma wouldn't be in the kitchen waiting. I hesitated, then opened the door and started to get out.

He reached across and touched my locket, turning it over like a dog-tag, then let it fall against my collar-bone.

"Wanna go out sometime?" he asked, running his finger up to my ear, the little hollow behind my jaw. I nodded and shut my eyes, waiting, my hand on the latch, one foot on the wet gravel. But that was it.

He gunned the engine then and I slid out, glimpsing Ardith's head slumped against the glass as he spun away, spraying the fence with loose stones.

*

Nearly three weeks went by before I saw him again—twenty days, to be exact. Every day I counted them, trying to replay his voice—or what I could remember of it above the rumbling engine—and what he'd said about going out. Meanwhile there were still no openings at the bank—nothing till fall at the earliest, they said—so summer was unfolding much as we'd expected, long afternoons by the library and in the Five-and-Ten, Ardith and Cheryl-Lynn laughing and carrying on over the usual stuff, just as before. Except that after the night of the dance Ardith would sometimes fall into a cranky silence, Cheryl-Lynn following suit like a regular Simon-says. At least they quit being so mouthy—I knew that if I never mentioned Waynie, Ardith wouldn't bring up John Alec. Just as well, as weeks passed with still no sign of him, as if I'd dreamed up the whole thing. Except the feel of his finger on my neck—that wouldn't go away, no matter how much I tried convincing myself it was no big deal.

One afternoon (it must have been a Wednesday, since everything was locked up tight, even the library) I was waiting for Ardith on the steps; Cheryl-Lynn was off somewhere babysitting. I kept glancing at the clock on the post office, figuring she must have gotten sidetracked washing her hair or something. Maybe I looked lonely lounging around the steps by myself—nobody to nudge or duck behind when his car came tooling along beside the sidewalk.

"What's the matter?" he yelled. "Friends stood ya up or what? You wanna come for a ride?" So much for being ticked off—I went right over and hopped in.

I don't know why I did it—I'd spent so long trying to make myself think I'd just imagined that night in his car, just built it up out of nothing. God knows, since that night it seemed I'd stopped thinking straight.

"I wanna show you somethin'," he said, never mentioning not calling. "It's out by the lakes."

We took the Trans-Canada this time, the mountains ahead getting closer and closer, then pulled off along the channel, the dark green water aswirl with currents and whirlpools. After a while we came to an orchard, gnarled trees in a narrow clearing that stretched down to the shore. A dirt lane ran through it and we parked and started walking, without talking, the mountain like a solid green wall across the channel, a thick border of birches and firs on both sides of the orchard.

Near the shore was a cabin, a tiny white clapboard place with sagging lattice along the porch, a scrap of net curtain flapping in the window. Not a soul to be seen.

"My grandpa's land," John Alec said. "The camp's all that's left." He took the rotting steps a couple at a time, slouching under the sagging roof. Then he paused in the doorway, gazing out at the water, his face shaded black in the sun's glare. A hornet stirred, circling my head in the heat. I swatted it away.

"Won't getcha inside," he laughed, ducking under the broken bulb on the porch. He thrust his hand through the ripped screen and opened the door, holding it for me, his eyes light and expressionless, the colour of honey. I hesitated, the sun blanching my bare arms, the top of my head.

"Come on, Grace—I won't bitecha."

He had on a black t-shirt, ribbed with moisture under the muscles of his chest; the veins in his forearm popped as he reached up to push his hair out of his eyes. I climbed the steps and stood beside him, peering inside, feeling his hand come up and lift the lank strands of hair off my shoulders and let them fall. Propping the door with his foot, he pressed closer and kissed my mouth.

"Come inside where it ain't so hot," he said, and I took his hand.

Inside the cabin it was dim and musty, smelling vaguely of old food. There was a wooden table with beer bottles and dead flies on the worn oilcloth, and across from it a couch, the springs popping out. Off to one side hung a tattered plastic curtain strung up with clothespegs, behind it a rusty cot with a grey camp blanket tossed over it.

John Alec pushed the curtain back and lay down on the cot, his arms crooked behind his head. Bright sunlight fell from the small window above, spilling across his chest, but his face was shadowed.

"So," he said, grinning, patting the mattress beside him. I

sat down stiffly on the edge, the springs clanging under me. He reached for my locket, then the hem of my top, helped pull it over my head, the buttons still done up. I felt exposed and foolish in my bright white bra, his hands fidgeting with it. He pulled it up over my breasts, staring at me. I squeezed my arms together to cover myself.

"What's wrong?" he said, twisting a strand of my hair on his finger.

"What if somebody comes?"

He laughed. "Nobody'd come all the way out here." The elastic was digging into my armpits, the tops of my breasts, as his hands slid over my nipples.

"John Alec."

He stopped.

"What's wrong?" he said again, impatiently this time. He tugged at the back of my bra; I felt the elastic let go, my breasts giving way. He moved his face to my chest, cupping his hands around my breasts, lifting them, squeezing.

"Please," I said, but he didn't seem to hear, his hand moving down under my waistband now, faster and more urgent, his fingers groping, sliding through the nest of hair. I could feel my wetness, his fingers moving deeper. He closed his eyes, moaning softly, and undid his zipper, guiding my hand down, moving his hips slightly, waiting.

My hand touched it—ridged and throbbing, swollen like an injured thumb but *impossibly* big—and jumped away.

"Grace. . . ," he coaxed, breathing into my hair. "I won't hurtcha. I ain't gonna hurtcha. . . ."

I shut my eyes, my fingers closing around it, his hand between my legs moving gently. He yanked my skirt up over my hips, my bra dangling from my arms, and worked my underpants down over my thighs, my knees.

"Come on, Grace, come on," he kept saying. "You want it, you want it, I know you want it." He flipped me onto my back, the springs creaking, digging into my skin as he pushed it inside me, gently at first, then thrusting blindly until it felt as if all his weight was settled there, thrusting. The zipper of his jeans cut into my thighs; his hips moved faster, faster, till the pain was burning, until finally he let out a groan and fell against me, his face damp and hot against mine.

I felt a tear trickle down my face and drip off my chin. His hand came up, tracing the wetness on my cheek.

"It gets better, ya know. It'll be better the next time," he said softly.

"But we aren't even *going out* yet," I blurted, when I could finally speak.

He laughed, easing my bra down over my breasts.

"Nothin' wrong with havin' some fun," he said, kissing me and looping his arm under my shoulders, stroking the damp hair from my face.

"I knew you never done it before," he said, rolling onto his back. I glanced down at his penis, small and purple, curled over on itself.

"Man, I could stay here for ever," he sighed, closing his eyes, settling beside me. Lifting my hips I pulled up my underpants, the wetness between my legs now clammy and cold. *Too cold to be blood,* I hoped, wanting desperately to look.

"What if I get pregnant?" I said, the sound of it like shock waves in the musty air. But it seemed to have no effect on him.

"Don't worry," he said. "I'm gonna take good care of you."

"But what if—"

"Don't ya believe me?"

"Yeah, right," I said, tears starting again. "I wish I could—"

"Come 'ere," he said. "No shit, I mean it, I really do." He drew me against him, kissing me softly. We lay there till a draft started to come around the window, and the light outside shifted from yellow to blue.

"It must be suppertime," I finally said. "Ma will be having a fit. . . ." I reached for the rest of my clothes; he stood and zipped up his jeans. And as I pulled on my top he reached for my locket, fumbling with the clasp.

"Lemme see," he said. "I wanna see it for a second."

I took it off and dropped it in his palm, the tarnished chain dangling through his fingers.

He put it in his pocket, then reached down to straighten the blanket.

"A reminder," he said. "For when we ain't together."

And I put my arms around his waist, my face against his smooth back.

"Okay."

Keeping House

Once we got off the dayliner John Alec knew exactly where to go—he'd been in Halifax before, he said, visiting his cousin. So I could see I was in good hands, but then I would have followed him anywhere.

We didn't get there till after supper. The sky was that soft blue that hints the days are getting longer. Stepping to the platform, you could see your breath mixed with the pee-tinged steam hissing from the tracks. And out beyond the girdered roof, rows and rows of railcars, freight sheds and grain elevators against the pale stars. Not a wisp of fog, though that was the first thing people mentioned if they'd ever been to Halifax—the fog. Gripping John Alec's arm, I took a deep breath, hoping for a whiff of the harbour. What I got was diesel.

John Alec took our bags and guided me through the crowded station, the clusters of people outside, towards some taxis waiting at the curb. He dropped our things—to flag down a driver, I figured—but after a second picked them up again, sliding his arm around my waist.

"You're gonna love it, Gracie," he said, steering me past the traffic. I smiled, thinking how stringy my hair must look from travelling all day.

We crossed a square with empty bottles in the bushes, a man on a bench talking to himself. I tried walking faster but my legs felt suddenly heavy, as if I'd *walked* all the way from Cape Breton.

"I feel like a bloody pioneer," I tried to joke, as we started up a hill. John Alec grinned.

"It's gonna be fine, you'll see," he said, stroking my hair back. Clinging to him, I wished he would kiss me, even a quick peck on the cheek. But he kept going, past the houses staged uphill. It started getting dark, dirty slabs of ice melting in silver trickles along the pavement, yellow lights blazing from windows. I wondered how things were going back home—people washing dishes, maybe, or cleaning their teeth. I pictured Ardith getting ready to go out with Cheryl-Lynn to bingo, Ma and Arch home watching the news, everyone going about their business same as always, as if I were still there. Suddenly Blackett seemed light-years away, another place entirely with no relation to me, as though the planet had shifted, my own life tilting off on its own. Adrift, I guess you could say. Except I was sure—well, pretty sure—that everything would turn out all right. John Alec would see that it did.

"Nothin' to be scared of," he said near the top of the hill. Then he leaned over and kissed me.

"I know." I smiled, following him around a corner, down a short street full of big houses somewhat shabbier than the ones on the hill. His cousin's street, I thought, grabbing his hand. The air was ripe with the smell of dog dirt thawing.

"Is this where she lives?"

"Who?" He looked at me and laughed. "Oh. *Geraldine*. Dunno where she lives these days."

"But I thought. . . ."

"She wouldn'ta had room anyway. . . ."

"Just one night. . . ?"

Tugging my sleeve, he started walking faster. I almost had to run to keep up, wearing only shoes—the blackpatent slingbacks Ma had bought me for business school. I pictured her putting away the supper dishes and a hollowness swelled inside me.

"Where we gonna sleep then?"

Only a couple of blocks long, the street was dead still but

for the ticking streetlights and a far-off rumble. A cat leapt out of the darkness and skittered away. Then from somewhere I could hear drunken voices, someone staggering behind us down the broken sidewalk.

"It ain't much further—I knows a place they always got rooms," John Alec said calmly.

With this my heart seemed to shrivel, but I looped my arm through his, counting up in my mind the times he said he'd been to Halifax.

"You'll feel better after ya get some sleep." He squeezed my arm under his elbow.

"What?" Finding a place to sleep seemed as likely as running into Ardith or Cheryl-Lynn.

"Wait'll we get to bed."

I bit my lip, trying hard to smile.

On the train I'd have laughed and told him to stop—not meaning it, of course. Not after being squished together all day on a sticky seat, a woman and her kids across from us, staring. Near Iona John Alec had put his head on my shoulder and dozed off, his hand on my leg while he slept. I'd imagined it travelling up my thigh, the warmth of it there almost making me sick with wanting him, and wishing it were the night coach. I'd let my desire drown out everything else.

Ma's nagging, for instance, when I told her what I was doing. "I'm going there for secretarial, you'll see," I said, giving the table an extra wipe so I wouldn't have to look at her.

"We'll see how far ya get," she sniffed, then sighed. "You think ya know him, but you wait and see. Ya can't trust a fella, not like that. When I was yer age—"

"Things are different now, Ma."

"People's still the same."

"Ma—"

"Don't say I never warned ya."

I tried telling her John Alec wasn't what she thought— that he was the type always kept a promise—but it was as if her mind was made up even before she met him.

"John Alec *loves* me," I yelled—my last words before running off to meet him at the station. Ma was out in the yard in just a sweater, checking the forsythia for buds. Never mind there was still snow on the ground.

"Plenty of work and stuff to do in Halifax," John Alec said, his arm around me in the tiny, brown waiting room. Mr. Hinch, the ticket agent, kept staring up at us from his glass wicket.

"For the two of us," John Alec said, handing over some money he'd got from selling his car. Mr. Hinch cleared his throat, his chins jiggling as he stamped the tickets "one way", his eyes avoiding ours. I suppose he wondered why nobody was there to see us off. By the time we heard the whistle wavering like an accordion through the woods behind Blackett, I was chomping at the bit to get moving and let the clickety-clack drown out the sound of Ma's voice.

Before we crossed the strait, John Alec woke and asked me to marry him. Just like that, with no to-do, no flowers or bent knee, the woman across from us taking it all in, smirking, then pointing at something out the window. I was so stunned that the rest of the trip is fuzzy, John Alec reaching for me when he thought the woman wasn't looking, some wild groping when she finally got off.

*

Near the end of Church Street was a grey house with two doors and an orange sign in the window. Furnished cold-water flat, lights not included, said the man who came to the door in an undershirt. He didn't ask if we were married, didn't so much as glance at my left hand. He just grunted when John Alec handed him some money—*my* money this time, from the five hundred dollars I'd saved up for Miss Murphy's Business College—and told him he'd have more by the first of the month. The man said we could move in any time.

"See?" John Alec said, testing out the mattress on the bedroom floor. "Told you things would work out." He didn't notice the mouse droppings under the kitchen sink, the rust-coloured stains around the toilet.

"A *shared* bath?" I whimpered. (A week would pass before I'd sit on the toilet seat.)

"Think you're the only one in the world who shits?" he laughed, jamming clothes—greyish underwear, some jeans and a couple of shirts—into the wobbly dresser. Then he came over and drew me to him, and we lay down on the stained mattress. He started tugging at my blouse.

"I thought you wanted to sleep," I yawned. My suitcase was still by the door, untouched. There seemed so much to do, I hardly knew where to begin. My eyes felt twitchy and raw from the bright ceiling light.

John Alec got up and turned it off, the glare from the street light pouring in through the bare window. He struck a match to light a cigarette; the draft put it out.

"It ain't for ever, right?" He took off his shirt.

I sat on the edge of the mattress—at least with the light out you couldn't see the dirt—and rubbed my hands together.

"And we got everything we need," he went on. Which was true, sort of. The flat had everything but sheets and dishes—a hotplate to cook on, an oil range for heat.

I got up and stumbled to the kitchen. From the window you could just see the harbour behind the rooftops, lights glimmering on the black surface. John Alec came in and started rubbing my back.

"It smells in here," I said, and he poked around the stove, shrugging at the stain where some oil had leaked onto the floor. I went to the front room and sat on the sagging couch. The smell was everywhere, clinging to the damp cushions and the limp curtains, even to my hair. After a while John Alec came and sat beside me.

"Whatcha thinking about, Gracie?" He ran his hand up my back, under my blouse.

"Nothing," I said, hunching over, shutting my eyes. Pictures crawled through my head of Ma washing her face and combing out her hair for bed. Arch too, up in his room reading magazines, calling *G'night* when he heard her light go out. If he was home, that is, and not out on a tear with his buddies.

"Come to bed," John Alec finally said, so we went and lay down on the bare mattress with our jackets for covers. It made me itchy wondering who else had slept there, but the feeling went away as John Alec pulled me close and started kissing me, his tongue gliding over my teeth.

Next morning we found a grocery store and bought supplies, mostly cleaning things, and I spent the rest of the day scrubbing and scouring. John Alec went out around lunchtime, looking for work, he said. He returned with a newspaper just before supper, which was tinned beans and Wholesome bread.

"Well?" I said.

"Loads of work," he sighed, his feet in my lap as he spooned up his beans. "I ain't worried."

"What about us?" I said, reaching over to stroke his cheek, my fingers scratchy and red from cleaning.

"Yeah?"

"What you asked me on the train."

"You go get the licence," he laughed, pushing away his plate and reaching for me.

"Aren't you hungry?"

"Starvin'," he said, kissing me.

*

We'd been settled in a month or so when John Alec got up one morning and suggested we go to City Hall and make things official. The ice was just about gone off the sidewalks, so I put on my good shoes, the ones I'd worn on the train, and my good skirt and blouse. We held hands walking down Barrington Street, past the junk shops and lunch counters, the churches and jewellery stores, John Alec hurrying along as if he were anxious to get things done. Like going to have a needle or a tooth pulled, I teased him. He said it was nerves, was all.

At City Hall we followed the signs to the basement and stood in line at the counter. They told us there was a waiting period after you got the licence—just as well, I told myself, since we needed to find witnesses.

A couple in the downstairs flat ended up standing for us —Garnet and Linda, I think their names were. Not friends exactly, and I suspect they only did it for the free drinks afterwards. (But then they didn't *have* to do it, and as John Alec said we didn't have much choice, with his cousin long gone and not a soul around we knew.) The vows were short and to the point, and everything went without a hitch except for the judge calling him Jim Alex once or twice. Nobody thought to snap a picture, though the people ahead of us had a photographer—the bride's father I think it was.

Afterwards Garnet and Linda came upstairs and we drank some Baby Duck, he and John Alec standing around smoking while Linda and I sat on the couch discussing meatloaf. Not that she looked like the type who cooked much. But I was so happy it seemed nothing could touch me that day, not even when Garnet glanced around the bare room and said, "Mind if I spin a disk, so we can dance a bit?"

Linda quit talking mid-recipe while John Alec clapped him on the back, waving his plastic wineglass.

"We only just moved in. But *my wife* here, she got all the money. So listen, the next time ya comes over we'll have a real party." But that was the last we saw of them; the next week there was somebody new downstairs.

For a wedding present Ma wired us a hundred dollars, which we spent on a set of orange-flowered sheets plus another month's rent while John Alec kept looking for work. As for other home improvements (as John Alec waited and waited to get on at the dockyard), I tried being as careful as I could with my money, stretching it as far as it would go on rent and groceries. Sometimes I'd do without myself so we could have the odd little treat, a case of beer, something like that. Though in truth I wasn't much of a drinker.

As it turned out, it was my savings we lived off all those months before John Alec finally got on at Pier 3. By the skin of his teeth, too, hanging around the cargo sheds every morning at six whenever a ship came in that needed unloading. They took him on in July, and just in time, with the baby due in December. He bragged about getting on in the slow season, while the Seaway was taking all the business. Mostly I felt relieved, especially when he joked about living on our looks all those months. It wasn't far from the truth—I'd lost ten pounds, I learned the day I went to the doctor and found out I was pregnant.

His first day at work, John Alec came home covered head to toe in tapioca flour, a pulled muscle in his side from lifting burlap bales. As my belly grew, there were times I couldn't stand being close to him, depending on the type of cargo he'd been moving. For a whole week he'd smell of rubber, for another of oranges. Some days it was enough to turn my stomach, even with the early months of morning sickness long past.

But I was still crazy in love, though by the time John Alec started working my savings were out the window and with them my plans for school. When Ma wrote and asked how it was going, I said Miss Murphy's had a waiting list and I'd apply next year. I never did tell her the truth—never had to, as it turned out, once I got pregnant. *There,* I thought with relief, *now I don't have to explain myself any more.*

I figured John Alec would be thrilled. But the truth is, he went to the tavern the day I found out and never came home till dawn the next morning. Maybe that's when things started to go sour; at first I told myself it was his nerves, getting used to his new job. But the bigger I got, the more it seemed he'd be off with his buddies, whoever they were. Stevedores from the Lighthouse Tavern, as far as I knew.

I decided to broach the subject one night after bringing Nancy home from the hospital. "If she can't have her daddy around, couldn't she at least have someplace decent to live, someplace with a yard, a bit of grass? You're making good money."

"Gracie, she don't barely have her eyes opened yet," he laughed. "Chrissakes, it's the middle of winter, whaddya need a yard for anyway?" That's how much he knew about babies.

When I went into the bedroom and lay on the bed with Nancy, he came and stood in the doorway.

"Look. I don't see what ya want a bigger place for. She don't do nothing but sleep, for Chrissakes. Whaddya think I'm made of, Gracie? Ya think money grows on trees? Jesus!" he shouted. As I stroked Nancy's wrinkly forehead, I told myself he was just trying to be responsible, worrying about money like that.

*

John Alec picked up a stroller a couple of weeks later at a thrift shop on Barrington Street. "A steal," he said with grim pleasure as he dragged it upstairs, the wheels leaving dirty puddles on the steps.

"It's been used," I said, eyeing the torn plastic. I just didn't feel right putting a new baby in it, not knowing where it had been or what children might've drooled on it. John Alec shoved it through the doorway, his features hardening in anger.

"What's the matter with you?" he began to yell. "Thing's like fuckin' brand-new. What, you scared whoever owned it's gonna see it and come after ya on the street? Well, I got news for you, Gracie. Nobody here gives a *squat* who you are or what you're doin'. Not one goddamn soul, you hear me?" He shook his head at me as if I were from Mars.

"I do," I said quietly, warming up soup on the hotplate. He didn't seem to be listening. "It's just that I want things nice for her," I tried explaining, setting his bowl in front of him. I sat down, nudging the wheels with my foot.

"She don't know the difference," he kept ranting, going to the fridge for a beer. "She don't know shit yet."

In the bedroom Nancy started to whimper, so I went and lifted her from the crib, my thumbs under her arms, my fingers holding her scrawny neck. She was so delicate, her downy head wobbling like a dahlia on a skinny stem and her little red face screwing up into a howl. I was still scared to death about picking her up, afraid one bad move and she'd break. I cradled her awkwardly on my shoulder, her head tucked like a peach under my chin. "Shhhhh," I crooned in a shaky voice, rubbing my lips against her scalp. "Come see what Daddy gotcha."

I brought her into the kitchen and set her down slowly into the stroller, trying hard to be gentle. Still her tiny limbs flopped against the plastic, her chin sinking into her chest like an old man's. She looked lost in there, but I did up the strap anyway, tight as it would go, then rolled and jiggled the stroller by its rusty handle. John Alec slumped at the table, picking off the label on his Keith's. Nancy opened her mouth and began to cry, her toothless gums in a quivering O, *a-waaaah, a-waaaah*, that newborn cry as if she'd been abandoned.

Running around like a machine, I dropped bottles into a pot of boiling water. One of the yellow nipples slipped from my fingers and rolled under the table; when I picked it up it was covered in dust. Nancy was screeching by then, flat in the stroller with her legs out stiff as broomsticks, the strap up around her armpits.

"Can't ya do something about that?" John Alec yelled, slamming down his half-finished beer. Then he grabbed his jacket off the doorknob and left, banging the door behind him.

That made the baby scream louder, while the water boiled over and spat on the burner. My hands shook as I stuck the nipple under the tap and then threw it in with the bottles, fiddling with the knobs on the hotplate. "Shhhh, shhhh, I'm coming, I'm coming," I kept pleading, tears rolling down my face as I shook the canned milk and corn syrup together. When I finally got the bottle to her mouth—her cheeks sucking in and out like bellows, her chest still heaving—her dark newborn eyes were steady with anger. And trust, I thought, a hateful, *terrifying* trust.

When Nancy finished feeding, I changed her diaper and dressed her in the pink knitted set Ma had sent. I imagined Ma's knobbed fingers fumbling with the yarn, *knit one purl one.* Then I bundled her in her fuzzy pink bunting bag and stuck her in the stroller, some rolled-up towels tucked around her head, and carefully, carefully as if I were moving an egg, carried it down both flights of stairs to the street.

There was a broken beer bottle on the sidewalk, and a stain that looked like blood. I swerved around it, the wheels sticking in the crusted snow. I'd forgotten gloves, but kept going, my sleeves tucked down over my fingers, pushing with all my weight to the end of the street. Then I headed towards the broader streets uptown, where rooming-houses gave way to large, well-painted homes with potted plants and dark furniture in the windows, rooms that looked unlived-in. People scooted past, their heads down in the blistering cold. The wind made Nancy blink and I waited for her to start screaming again, turning sharply down South Park Street till the icy blast from the harbour was behind us. By the Public Gardens she drifted off and I slowed down a bit, watching the ducks huddled like curling stones in the snow, the laughter of children in a playground across the street ringing above the clang of trolleys, sparks snapping in the wires overhead.

I wondered where John Alec had taken off to. But glancing down at Nancy's sleeping face, I felt oddly restful, relaxed in a way I hadn't been for weeks, especially not since her birth. *She's three weeks old,* I thought, as if it were some kind of landmark—not for her but for me, that I'd survived things this far. Not so much with John Alec, as without Ma. And pushing the stroller between the snowbanks back to Church Street, it hit me how very far I was from her, and how there could be no going back to her, not now or ever.

Knocked out by the cold, Nancy was still asleep when I dragged the stroller upstairs. I left her bundled up in it, the slushy wheels melting all over the hall linoleum as I went to the kitchen and made myself some tea. I managed to get a whole fifteen minutes to myself, just staring out at the big green oildrums along the blue and white waterfront, sea-smoke swirling off the water like something in a movie. Then I heard John Alec come in, and remembered he'd want his supper early since he was starting the late shift that night.

*

For the rest of the winter I got into the habit of taking Nancy out after lunch, as long as it wasn't too cold and the sidewalks were shovelled. John Alec was working double shifts, the port in full swing with the Seaway frozen. He liked to catch up on his sleep in the afternoons, said he slept better if Nancy's crying didn't disturb him. As for *us*—well, with him working all hours there wasn't time to talk, let alone fight. Though when we did get together it usually ended up in that back-and-forth of two people talking, neither listening, till sometimes I wondered how we'd ever gotten together in the first place.

So I wasn't really prepared one day when I came in from walking the baby, huffing a little from carrying the stroller. He was waiting at the top of the stairs—I braced myself for him to start growling about me not being there to start supper. But he grinned instead, reaching down to help with the stroller.

"What's yer rush?" he said. I could smell the beer off him as he tugged at my coat.

I wiped the dampness off my forehead; my blouse stuck to me from struggling upstairs. Nancy's eyelids fluttered open and she started to whimper.

"Come here," he said, pulling me to him. "She's not gonna starve or nothing."

I broke from him and picked the baby up, patting her back as she sucked on her fist.

"Jesus Christ," he muttered, disappearing into the bedroom.

While I was feeding her I heard him come out and pause

for a second on the landing.

"Don't bother cookin'," he yelled.

"Wait a minute," I yelled back, but when I got up he was gone. He didn't come home until after I was asleep.

*

About a month later he was waiting for us again when we got home. The weather had started warming up, which meant Nancy didn't have to be quite so bundled up. Plus she could hold her head up and look around, smiling at everything in sight. When we met him at the door he was smiling too, holding his thumb out for her to suck on. She wrapped her fist around it and pulled it to her mouth, and he started laughing, as if he wasn't sure what to do next.

"What's wrong?" I asked.

He laughed till the muscles under his shirt started heaving.

"Bunch of us gettin' laid off," he said, beaming like he'd won a goddamn lottery. "So we're goin' to Ontario. Plenty of work up there, jobs jobs jobs, doin' anything ya want." I felt like slapping him, just to get that grin off his face.

"When are we going?" My heart felt as if it were seizing up —we'd only just gotten used to *this* place, with its grey streets and fog, the constant fog like salty wool. It was like being told I was expecting again, the fat from Nancy still loose around my middle.

"Bunch of us leavin' next week," he said, lifting the baby and shoving the stroller into a corner.

"But what about *us!*"

"I'll send ya the money once I'm workin' and youse can take the train up."

"When?"

"Whenever."

"I see," I said, meaning I knew there was no point arguing.

*

It's September now—the air has that faded warmth that makes me think of chalkboards and new shoes. A group of young people passes Nancy and me on the sidewalk, bright pennies in their loafers, their notebooks flapping. Maybe they're going to the university, or else one of the high schools, I'm not sure which. Nancy gurgles and points at a leaf on the ground. One of the students glances back at her for a second and keeps going. A wheel on the stroller starts to shimmy, so I slow down, Nancy twisted backwards still reaching for the leaf. I *won't* run back to grab it for her.

John Alec has been gone seven months; I've just turned nineteen.

More students come up behind us—they stop talking as if to tell me to hurry up. Careful of the loose wheel, I pull Nancy to the side into the scuffed dirt, the camomile springing up like dusty hair. Behind me crickets are going like buzz-saws, a sound that makes me wonder where the summer's gone. Next comes a couple holding hands—the girl looks so young, though she must be sixteen, her bare calves tensing as she hurries along with her boyfriend. Nancy squirms and holds out her arms for me to pick her up. If not for the baby, I would feel invisible.

A cheque for two hundred dollars came this week, the third or fourth since John Alec went away. I know they're from him because his name is on the bottom. There's never a note, though, or a return address on the envelope, just the Toronto postmark. Maybe he hasn't found an apartment yet; could be he's still staying with the fellows he drove up there with. A couple of times the phone has rung—nobody there when I picked it up. One time a woman called looking for him, but she hung up when I asked was she Geraldine, his cousin.

I think of John Alec late at night, lying there trying to get back to sleep after Nancy's woken me up. Though I remember his voice, I have trouble seeing his face—not his features, but the sum of them. I wonder if he has the same problem picturing me. But mostly I wonder, will Nancy know him when she sees him again?

Home Fires

On Tuesdays I clean the house top to bottom, whether it needs it or not. I start at the kitchen sink, scrubbing off the tea stains, then work my way upstairs, dusting and scouring. A light sweep of the bedrooms, the parlour—the least-used rooms—saving the bathroom and the blue-stained tub for last. Gives me something to do with the place empty—a body can only bake so many pies and squares and loaves of bread. Then there's Archie's room—he's been gone ten days now. Today I'll give his room a proper going-over, now I'm finally up to it. Figure I'd better make up for all the years I couldn't get past his door, let alone give the place a good scrubbing. If I don't do it now I never will.

The morning he left for Ontario I climbed the attic stairs with the dry mop and started under his bed. Wads of dust like hairballs the cat brings up, grey fur mixed with the sandy strands of Archie's hair. Tied a clean rag over the mop and knocked down the cobwebs hanging like beards from the ceiling. Looked like the room had been vacant for years, though God knows the hours Archie spent holed up in there once he left the garage.

"Why don'tcha go uptown and see what the other fellas are doin'?" I'd ask, but he'd just moan. "Aww, Ma, they're all wrapped up with the girlfriends these days." So I could see he had no interest, no interest at all in his old friends. It was like having a bit of gravel in my shoe, knowing he was up there moping around all day. Not doing much of anything besides lolling on the bed with his shoes on, reading magazines, day in and day out. As for the mess in his room—it wasn't that I was slack so much as the fact he was always in it.

Even as he was backing his green Ford onto the road, looking hard into the side mirror with a cigarette clenched in his teeth, I was thinking how I'd go in and get the Mr. Clean and the new yellow bucket hanging in the porch once he was gone. To take my mind off things. Yes, as I stood at the gate waving, waving till my shoulder ached, I was thinking how I'd polish the banister in the hall, wipe down the taps in the bathroom, maybe do under the beds in the boys' old room. Then on to the attic and Archie's den. I had it all planned how I'd go up and sort through his closet, clear out some of the junk. Those greasy black boots from his old job, that boxful of spark plugs and fan belts, the rubber dry and cracked like stretched liquorice. I'd take down the faded blue curtains and wash them, run a dust-rag over the baseboards, the windowsill. I was thinking how much bigger the room would look without the clutter as I watched the car burble down the street, picking up speed in front of Pritchard's dairy. *Keep busy, keep busy,* I kept telling myself. It was better than wishing I was in that car too. Like his guardian angel, as the Catholics say. Never mind the boy's nearly twenty-five years old.

In front of Pritchard's Archie slowed down, almost to a stop, and for a minute my heart jumped. Maybe he was changing his mind, deciding Blackett wasn't so dead-end after all. I quit waving, standing there in the dust with my hands folded inside my apron. Praying. But then I saw Pritchards' grandson drag his trike out of Archie's way and over to the dairy steps. I heard Archie honk the horn, just once, and then he was gone. Leaving me with my cleaning, and all the time in the world. Time I would've killed for, other points in my life.

Ten days. The first time I've been alone in this house, not counting those early months Thomas was working double shifts at the bankhead, before my first was born. To me those days don't count, since I was happy enough making his bed and his meals, watching my belly grow. Forty-odd years since Thomas brought me here, a sweet-faced bride. Lordy, I was green! But that soon changed, after the first one came, then the second, and the third—a new one just about every year, nine months to the day after things like Christmas and church picnics. Nine babies in all, not counting two that didn't live. What a woman gets sucked into, having so many kids—your life flies past like a train with no stops when you're used to a full house. Or at least one other body—even if it *is* layin' prone behind a door, no sound but pages flipping.

"Whatcha readin'?" I always asked when Archie came downstairs for more tea or to clean the clinkers out of the stove.

"Nothin' much," he'd say, rooting around the cupboard for a fresh can of milk. I just assumed he was reading about cars, since cars seemed all Archie cared about from the time he could talk. Even his pa—poor Thomas—would laugh and say, "Well, he's a real Cape Bretoner then—got to have a car, never mind if ya don't own a pot to piss in. You can drive a car, Het, but ya can't drive a house." Oh, Thomas used to joke about it, but I don't think he was entirely laughing. Thomas's father was from the mainland, so his people weren't true islanders, not like others around here.

With his love of driving and all, it surprises me Archie stayed home this long. *Lucky to have had him as long as I did,* I think now, as I stand in the pantry working lard into some flour for apple pies, the last thing before I head upstairs. The rolling-pin thuds against the counter, flour dusting the brown-painted floorboards. Ten days and not a word, not even one quick phone call. *What, they don't have phones wherever it is you are?* I slice apples for three pies—another church tea-and-sale—though the ladies' auxiliary only asked for one. The dough crusted in my fingernails is a comfort, like the dried-salt tightness of your skin after a dip in the ocean. The comfort of something done a thousand times before. I measure the cinnamon, just enough sugar.

Take it easy, the ladies say. *Have a rest now the young fella's finally out of yer hair. You got it coming to ya, Hettie. Enjoy the time to yerself—get out more. Someplace further afield than church or the co-op store. Now the last of yer brood has flown the coop. And not a bit too soon—that last one took some time leavin'.*

Truth is, I don't know where to start. When I finish the pies I sweep up the flour, and while they're baking I'll get started on Archie's room. Give it some elbow-grease this time. Because that's what I do Tuesdays. Mondays I do the wash, Tuesdays dust and sweep, Wednesdays scrub, Thursdays bake. Saturdays too, and any other day the need arises. And cook: Friday boiled cod, Sunday a roast of beef, Monday a crock of beans. Even when the others started moving away—all seven boys, before Archie and Grace, my baby—I kept cooking. The same things, just smaller amounts. Using the same old speckled pots, hardly needing to follow a recipe. A lot of it I could've done in my sleep. Till finally Grace said: "You're gonna make me fat, Ma." Archie, though, always appreciated my cooking. Three times a day, on the dot. Archie in his spot beside the window, from the time he was a stick of a thing in the old spool highchair. Lord, it seems just last week I was wiping porridge off his fat fingers and pointy little chin, those wide blue eyes watching me. A grown man now, gone off to look for work the way all his brothers did—out west, all over kingdom come—and Grace down in Halifax with a husband and a baby of her own.

I never thought Arch would leave me. *Not right, a big man like that livin' off his mama.* I know that's what the whole town was thinking, even the clerk in the co-op watching me count out the money for a tin of corned beef, a head of lettuce. For a long time I kept my head bowed, feeling their thoughts jumping like sparks. *Too damned lazy to go out an' support himself. Takin' advantage of his poor mother, an old widow.* As if I had no say in any of it, as if I've gone soft since Thomas died. *Havin' all those kids took the backbone out of 'er. No wonder she's limp as a dishrag, far as the young fella's concerned.*

Soft, *indulgent.* They think I've been too easy on him, that my softness is contagious and Archie's like a cranberry left too long in the bog, deep wine-red but a pulpy mess when you go to pick it. Best left for the birds. *Good for nothin', lazy son-of-a—* But what they don't know is how I've felt seeing so many go. Sure, there's not a mother on this island hasn't had a young one leave for Halifax or Boston, Toronto or the west. And in some ways I wouldn't wish it otherwise. But those other mothers, they act like they're proud. *My girl's workin' for the government now and doin' right good for herself. Yup, the young fella's got a job makin' cars in Oshawa or Windsor, somewheres in Ontario. An' he's got the wife, the kids, a pool in the backyard. Imagine that, now, if ya will.* What they don't say is how they felt the night before, making up a stack of sandwiches, wrapping them just so with wax paper new off the roll, not saved from the day before. Trying to look cheerful and busy, while they're chewing their lips to keep from sobbing.

I've lost seven sons that way, different times. I have a hard time now keeping them separate, remembering exactly who's where, their big ruddy faces all blurred into one. Seven of them, strung all over the country. Gone but for the letters they write, the money they send home at Christmas or my birthday. *Buy yourself something, Ma.* I don't want their money. But I've got quite a pile of crisp new tens in the Pot of Gold box on my dresser. The last couple of years I've dipped into it to send something to Grace for her birthday, or her little girl's, which she always thanks me for. But with fancy little cards, never more than a note.

When Archie was leaving I stuffed a wad in with his sandwiches. I know he would've turned it down if I'd mentioned it. *It's your money, Ma. I don't wanna take it.* Truth is, I wouldn't know where to spend it in this town, except on a card of needles, a packet of hairnets, a plastic rain bonnet, a yard or two of cotton. The only things beside groceries I ever buy. There's not much I need nowadays, at my age. And anyway the bills seem too fresh to spend. Looking at them makes me think of the boys—Fulton, Murdoch, Albert, Donald, Tommy,

Dan and Joseph—cashing their paycheques, folding the money into their wallets and setting aside the newest notes for me. But I prefer not to think how they earn them. I nursed Thomas to his death-bed—lung cancer—and he never worked below ground, spent thirty years overseeing the machine shop. Oh, he'd come home a little dusty, but never so's you couldn't recognize him. But no, I can't bear to think of my boys black-faced, nothing but their eyes and the pink of their tongues to mark them from the next fellow, walking hunchbacked the rest of their lives. Like animals, really, tuned to the sounds of water dripping, the darkness of a tomb. But that's how they've chosen to earn their living. And this is why I've never pushed Archie. Not even when people said *Young fella like that, what's he doin' at the garage? Money's a hell of a lot better at the pit.* No, from the minute Archie slid out of me into the doctor's arms, and afterwards gazing into his dark infant eyes, I knew I'd never let my Archie go into the mine.

I untie my apron and start up the steep, narrow stairs, my hand flat against the wainscot to steady myself. At the landing a tiredness comes over me—I realize I've been awake since dawn, for no reason besides habit. I've been trying to sleep more to pass the time. *Relax, relax. Stop wearin' yourself thin. Now's your chance to slow 'er down a bit.* Before I start up the attic stairs I stop at my room and look in, everything neat as a pin. Rankles a bit to think I've *liked* it so tidy: my own little temple, no kids allowed. The way Thomas used to keep me in bed till nearly nine some Saturday mornings, the door locked and the skeleton key on top of the dresser. Lord knows what the boys got into downstairs while we lay there naked, sun blazing around the dark green blind. Before I ever thought of Archie or Grace, my two surprises, one after the other.

Now the whole house is like my room—spotless and orderly as a church, not a thing out of place. Too neat, everywhere but Archie's room. Which is why it's taken me so long to go back up there and finish what I started. Bundle up the magazines for the hospital, see if those fan belts are any good to anybody.

Maybe someone could use them. And those old boots. But no, it's early yet to be going through his clothes.

Once I catch my breath I continue upstairs, open the door to the little room. It's cramped and musty, the ceiling sloped over the narrow bed with its sugar-bag quilt, a new sifting of dust on everything. I run a damp rag over the piles of stuff on his dresser, the metal knobs on the bedposts. Grey fluff has started to gather under the bed again—dirt must rise to the top of a house. The air is like cold stew, the dampness drummed in by the mossy patter of rain on the shingles. Shortness of breath makes me sit down hard on the jiggling mattress, and I roll down the sleeves of my work blouse, looking around at the leaf-patterned wallpaper. A stain like a rusty fern has spread under the eaves. Archie could've had the big room next to mine, after Dan and Joe went to British Columbia. But he said he didn't want to disturb me.

I work off my slippers and stretch out, jangling the springs. I try to shut out the gloom, the smell of mildew and rotten wood, a smell it seems no amount of scouring can remove. It was all through the place when Thomas first brought me here from my home by the foundry. After a while it went away—or the smell of diapers covered it up.

I've always hated this house. It's always seemed topsy-turvy, the kitchen at the bottom and the parlour above, like a poor man's idea of something grand. But I never complained. So many stairs, up and down, up and down. No wonder the youngest ones stayed put in the attic—I suppose it was their little refuge, forgotten, at the top of the house. When we came here from the church, my family oohed and ahhed about the wide hall upstairs and the polished banister, the deer's head over the coathooks. All except Mama, who sucked in her cheeks and said, "Lord, Lord, girl, all the stairs. Just wait till the babies start coming, you'll be fit to be tied then, Harriet."

As for me, I'd been hoping we'd get to live uptown, in Thomas's family home. The tall green house with the wide veranda, shaded with big heart-shaped leaves in the summertime, a nice barn out back for Thomas to putter. But no. Thomas's sister would have nothing to do with me, and as far as she was concerned it was *her* house, never mind that the old man left it to both of them. And Thomas, God forgive him, wanted to be closer to the pit. *Wouldn't do now, would it, for the men to think I lived up by the bosses?* He thought he was doing me a kindness, too, keeping me close to where I'd grown up. Poor Thomas, as pale a memory now as the foundry. Nothing left but the coke ovens, some brick arches sticking out of the alders, separated from the road by the swamp. *The poison pond*, the boys used to call it when they went down there to visit their granny. *Don't go near it or ya might fall in an' get yer legs burnt off!* I can't remember if it was me started saying that or the boys themselves. And by the time Archie and Grace came along both Mama and Papa were gone, the old house a ruin sagging into the ground, broken windows like empty eyes looking out on the fallen brickwork.

*

I awake with a queer jolt, as if I've fallen from a great height and struck the bed, still holding my dust-rag, not even aware I drifted off. The sound of rain has stopped. I get up and go over to the bureau, lift the pile of magazines to see what's buried beneath. The old tape recorder one of his brothers let him have, a new package of fuses. I set the magazines on the bed, start riffling through them, the glossy pages squeaking between my rough fingers.

Under the shiny covers they're not at all what I expect, which is pictures of cars, things about engines. The only photographs of automobiles are ads—the rest show women, pink-skinned young women in nothing but their underclothes, the curve of a large round breast popping out here, a small pink teat there. They look like dolls to me, plastic bodies too smooth and pink to be real. In spite of myself I turn more pages, faster. The magazine folds open to a woman with hair like yellow cotton candy, wearing nothing at all. I quickly look away, staring at my hands, raw-knuckled against the shiny paper, as if they don't belong to me.

I tuck the magazine carefully under the others and shove the whole works under the bed. I don't know why I'm shaking so, it's not like Archie's a child. I make myself stop long enough to smooth the quilt, slap the pillow into shape. *But he's such a good boy, so serious. Not like some other fellas his age, drinkin' and racin' up and down Main Street with girls snuggled close. No, Archie's too good for such foolishness. Which is why he had to get away.*

If I could just talk to him now, I think, if only he'd phone. It hits me how I haven't grieved like this since I lost Thomas. Not his death—a sting salved with relief—but before that, when I still longed for him the way he once was. A deeper wound, like the mined-out tunnels under the town, emptied, exhausted. The guts of the earth hollow, nothing but a crust of worn-out rock keeping the houses from caving in on themselves.

Gently I shut the door and go downstairs. The fire in the kitchen stove is all but out, rain stinging the windows again. I go to the scuttle in the corner and scrabble for the lumps left at the bottom. But instead of ducking out to the coalshed, I go into the dining room, dim as nightfall though it's not yet noon. I don't bother switching on the lamp, just sit for a while in the little padded rocker. It's cold and damp enough to peel the wallpaper. I pick up the telephone and dial Mrs. Pritchard down the street, the urge to hear another voice swelling like a breaker. *If ya ever need anything*, she's always saying, *if ya ever need anything*. It rings and rings, and after a few seconds I hang up and go over to the fireplace.

Beside the grate is an iron kettle full of shore coal, dull black nuggets like chestnuts. Archie collected it off the beach every time he took a swim last summer, enough for a fire at Christmas and then some. My knees creaking, I kneel on the hearth tiles and begin piling handfuls upon the grate. Once there's a neat mound I get up, my joints cracking with the dampness, and go to the kitchen for matches and yesterday's *Post*, a bit of kindling from the box behind the stove.

I kneel again on the cold tiles, crumpling paper, tucking it into the coal, then strike a match. Light warms the greyness. Flames leap, spreading slowly from the bits of paper to the coal, haloed with pale orange before it burns blue. I squat there, deaf to the pain in my legs. I hold my palms to the screen as brightness fills up the little room, pushing the gloom into the corners. Orange sparks glint in a glass bowl on the table, the rain falling in sheets now at the window, thrumming the garden outside. The coal burns steadily, slowly, a clean blue strength.

I have always loved a fire. It comes back to me how, surrounded by the clamour of children, I could find some quiet gazing into the flames. I could see things—stars. Then somebody would crawl up on my lap or clasp little stick arms around my neck, choking me with hugs. *Whatcha lookin' at, Mama? Nothin, oh nothin' a-tall.* They'd look at me worried, the way children do when they sense their mama's not all there. But now there's nobody hanging off my arms or my hips, the flames look exactly as they're meant to, nothing more. I've quit looking for shapes or patterns. I've forgotten about anything more than the feel of dry heat on my face, on my hands, simple comforts.

When finally I let the fire burn down, there are only a few chunks left in the kettle. The clock on the mantel whirrs out three. I poke the ashes, grey lumps which fall into dust. Then I climb the stairs again.

Without looking around, I pull the heavy black tape recorder off Archie's dresser and carry it back down to the dining room. I wipe the dust off, then plug it in and poke around to find the right button. Lord knows what Archie might have recorded—I can't recall him spending much time fussing over tapes. But I keep fumbling with the buttons till I get it working.

The voice jumps out, a cough, a sound like a chair being dragged over crusted snow. *Testing testing, one-two-three-four.* Archie's voice, and then whistling like the hiss of wind through a field of daisies, a tune I recognize. *Yankee doodle went to town a-riding on a po*— Another cough, a long pause, more scraping, then nothing but a furry sound and the little wheels squeaking around and around and around. I wait and wait for one more word, a whisper, the sound of him breathing. But nothing comes, nothing but the sharp click of the wheels stopping.

Any Night of the Week

"All the way up there? I don't see why ya have to go so far."
Ma was stirring a big potful of blueberry jam when I told her I
was leaving. I'd waited till she was in the middle of something
so she wouldn't pull off her apron and stomp upstairs after
me. Just in case she had something to say, though Lord knows
Ma was better at saying nothing, nothing at all. It was the look
in her eyes got you, the way she'd drop into the rocker and sit
with her arms folded, just looking at you.

"Why not someplace closer? Halifax—your sister's there,
and that cousin of Pa's—"

"No!" I cut her off. The ruckus out back from coal cars
switching tracks had made me raise my voice, made me feel
more determined to stand up to her.

"Plenty of work in Halifax!"

"No, Ma. It's real city lights I need to see." *And Halifax isn't
far enough away, Ma, not nearly far enough!*

She dipped the tin ladle into the pot, calm as if we were
talking about me going uptown for milk, everything as orderly
and deadly dull as usual. Then she started tipping hot blueberry
into the jars, wincing a little when it touched her fingers, all
inky under the nails.

How the hell could I explain that what I craved was a place
full of cars and strangers? Someplace you could go to a different
tavern every night and never worry about getting barred. Or
having it get back to your mother you were seen with some

loose woman. A fella could get buried alive messing on the wrong side of the tracks in Blackett, and I don't mean those poor suckers breaking their backs in the pit. No, what I wanted was to be someplace where loose women were as unmarked as proper ones, all fresh territory to navigate. I was just plain tired of being Ma's son.

"What in God's name do ya plan to do there anyway? We don't know a soul in *Toronto!*" The way she said it—as if the place were in another galaxy, beyond the Milky Way. They'd just put a man on the moon, for Chrissake.

"Why don'tcha see if they'll take ya back on at the garage?"

It was the last straw—I knew she wouldn't like it, but I never expected *that.* So I went upstairs, dragged Pa's old black suitcase out of the closet and started packing. While she was melting wax to seal the jars, before she could stop me.

See, I was used to her keeping mum. She'd hardly said a word the day I quit grade twelve to go full-time pumping gas. What the hell—I was one of the few fellas my age still in school anyway, the rest having left to work at the pit. *Get an education,* she was always harping, *somethin' nobody can take from ya.* She laid that on especially thick with Grace—having given up on the rest of us, I guess. But that morning I told her I was going to MacKiggan's garage instead of school, she looked like a doe on the centre line, eyes frozen in the headlights before it scats off into the bushes. Me dilly-dallying with the brakes.

To tell the truth, I'd been all geared up to defend myself—guess I've always been a little afraid of Ma—well, afraid at least of the look she gets. But she just slouched off to the pantry and got out Pa's old lunchpail, maybe glad to see it used after gathering dust so long under the cupboard. Old man gone fourteen years by then, worked his life away at the pit, above ground, a foreman. Guys at school used to razz me, say he wasn't a real miner like their fathers, crawling around on their hands and knees in the deeps. Everyone ends up six feet under eventually, so why in Christ's name spend your life down there too? *Education.* Ma never let up, not even passing the tinned-meat sandwiches after Pa's funeral. *Get yerself educated and you'll live longer. Spare everyone a lotta grief.*

When the job at MacKiggan's came up I thought, what the hell, it's not the pit, and even if I stay in school, where do most fellas end up? Thank the old man for that, for sticking around Blackett when the world could've been his oyster. He had family on the mainland, for Chrissake! And still he kept us here in this godforsaken town. So when they took me on at the garage I figured I was doing good for a fella with no trade. Regular straight wages, nothing taken off for doing the work itself. Not like guys I knew, docked part of a week's pay for the dynamite they used, and not a cent extra for the tons of rock they hauled out. MacKiggan's got me started, I'll give it that. Set me up with some wheels, and the taste for something better. A sea-green Ford in good shape, two hundred bucks cash in my billfold, not one red cent owing to nobody.

*

I was emptying out my top drawer, dumping some shorts and a couple of shirts into Pa's suitcase, when I heard her on the stairs, her wobbly gait on account of her bad knee. Next thing she was in the doorway, wringing her hands like towels.

"That musty old thing—ya might air it out first," she said as I rifled through the drawers, hardly noticing what I was grabbing.

"Suit yerself then," she sighed. I kept throwing things into the suitcase so I wouldn't have to look at her. "With all the rest gone, I guess it's yer turn now."

I took this as a blessing—though it was starting to seem too easy. Downstairs I could hear the hot lids on the jam popping. One after another, like buckshot.

"You're a grown man, Archie. Nothin' I can do to stop ya." Then she turned around and started for the stairs, breathing loud and raspy. "I got bread to bake," she muttered, teetering on the top step to put her good leg first.

"Wait a minute, Ma, I want ya to hear me out."

"Two loaves to do us the week, two more for the church sale."

"Chrissake, Ma. I'll go up to the bakery before I leave. It's not like you have to—" But I flopped down on the bed, seeing it was no use. Even with an empty house the woman would run herself into the ground, as if slowing down would allow the devil himself to creep up and nip her on the arse.

"I promised the auxiliary—" she said, all huffy.

"Ma, I can't stay in Blackett for ever."

"I know," she said, the steps creaking. "It's just that you're my last one." She stopped at the landing, turned her head back as she spoke.

"Ya should be use' to it by now." By God, she'd already seen Grace leave, her pride and joy, not to mention my seven brothers.

"Ya never get used to it, Archie."

And then she disappeared, though I could hear her downstairs thumping dough against the counter, rattling pans on the stove. She never asked when I was leaving or what my plans were. Good thing—I hardly knew myself.

When I came downstairs with the suitcase she was slumped in the rocker by the stove, picking dried dough out of her nails.

"You could at least wait an' get a good start in the mornin'. An' I could fix ya a decent lunch." She handed me a wrinkled paper bag.

Must've been nearly four in the afternoon when I went out and loaded the suitcase into the Ford. Ma started to sniffle, standing under the lilac bushes by the driveway, her face in the shadows. I bent down to brush a speck of mud off the fender, so shiny I could see myself in it, then jumped in and revved 'er up. She moved beside the car then, hands inside the bosom of her apron, her saggy bulk under the faded cotton all I could see of her.

"Don't cry, Ma," I wanted to say, but I knew it was no use. So I gunned it out of the yard, my eyes on the mirror. Around the corner I chucked the lunch out the window, glimpsed it rolling into the ditch.

As I steered out of town, past the dingy little storefronts and sagging porches, past the Grey school and the bank, along the road to the cemetery out on the cliff, it was as though years of my life were leaking out of me like oil from an engine. All those days and hours of wasted time since I'd left the garage flying away like exhaust. And funny thing, I never saw a soul, friend or foe, as I drove off, dark green mountains rising in the windshield, the rooftops of town shrinking behind me.

Foot to the floor I made it over the top of Kelly's Mountain, nothing below but the bright blue water of the lakes, the sea, and everywhere flat-topped mountains jutting off into purple. By the time the road levelled out among the hills above the Bras d'Or, I was doing eighty, no problem, and whistlin' Dixie. Blackett a smudge in my memory.

When I crossed to the mainland it was getting dusky, the hills behind me shadows. I almost stopped on the other side of the causeway for a smoke. But I thought of Ma's face and kept going, turning my back once and for all on the island and everything holding me to it. Not just Ma, but her parents and Pa too. All their kin, dust and bones in the black ground. So many arms, dead and alive, reaching out to pull me backwards. By the Jesus, they wouldn't have me—not till I'd had a life. So I drove all that night and all the next, till noon the following day I made it to Yonge Street, the shine of water out beyond the buildings. Block after block, all brick and asphalt and everything new. Quite a stretch from Blackett, where the potholes would tear the axle off a car. Kind of place Ma would've marvelled at, I thought, as the wide streets full of big brick houses gave way to ones rutted with streetcar tracks, jammed with cars blasting their horns.

The Ford was so covered with road dust I hardly recognized her reflection creeping past the plate-glass storefronts, the crowded sidewalks. The traffic thickened, cars crawling along like bugs, so I decided to take a left and before I knew it I was headed east along another road that seemed to go on for ever. Finally got turned around and went back towards Yonge, stopping a few blocks short outside a place called the Triple Nickel. "Rooms by the Week," said the sign on the chipped-tile front, and though I didn't like the look of the fellas hanging in the doorway, I parked as close as I could and walked back with Pa's suitcase. Leaning against the door was a big fella, spitting image of old Mickey Harris from Pit Street. As I opened my mouth to speak, he lunged for the suitcase, the others milling closer like they were fixing to beat the tar out of me. Then I saw he was so gassed up he could barely stand.

"Ya got a smoke, kid?" he said, and I tossed him one as I shouldered past. A grand introduction to the city of dreams, I thought, dragging the suitcase up to the bar.

"Any chance of a room for the night?" I asked the woman pouring draft.

"How much you wanna pay?"

I laid a bill on the counter.

"Up the stairs and to yer right."

The room was no bigger than a closet, with a rusty cot and a sink in the corner with somebody's dinner puked into it. Half a plastic curtain sagged at the window, which looked out on a sooty brick wall, more grimy glass, and everywhere the smell of piss. I was dog-tired from driving, but nothing could make me lie down on *that* bed. Not sober, anyway. So I slid the suitcase underneath and went downstairs for a few beers. To get my bearings.

The place was almost full, but I managed to find a spot in a corner away from the tables of the men, most of them Pa's age—old enough that I felt a bit ashamed of my youth, the swell of muscle under my wrinkled shirt. Some looked like men I knew from Blackett, but these faces had a kind of hunger or meanness I'd never seen before, or at least had never noticed. If fellas in Blackett seemed half-corked, these guys looked used up. The only sound some muddy guitar music coming from a jukebox—the Beatles singing "Revolution"—and men slouched over wobbly grey tables snoring in their beer, one with a trickle of blood from his nose. The woman behind the bar picked up her tray and came over, her flat shoes slapping the tiles.

"So what'll it be, pal?" She stood beside me, her brown uniform brushing my arm, one bony hand tapping the table. She hoisted the tray, shifting the weight to her other hip, so close I could smell her—sweat and beer and something else, like spoiled cheese.

"Come on pal—all's we sell is beer." She slammed down a couple of draft and I handed her another bill. Pinching her orange-painted lips together, she pumped change from the belt around her thick waist and dropped it on the table.

I took a few sips but to tell the truth I didn't feel much like drinking, surrounded by fellas more dead than alive, bumming smokes off each other in a dull growl. But I couldn't bring myself to trudge upstairs. So I sat there till it got dark outside, and then till closing time, the beer in my glass flat as piss. All the time trying not to wish I was somewhere else, having a few with the boys at Martinello's, getting tanked. Maybe breaking into a few foolish songs, egging the others on to jump on the table-tops till Georgie, the bastard, chucked us out. Girls outside, all dolled up for Saturday night, watching to see who'd be first to jump into the back seat. Oh my Jesus. And Ma next morning acting like she never heard a thing, me staggering in so loaded I'd miss the toilet, then pass out till all hours. Ma creeping around downstairs so as not to wake me.

The waitress ignored me the rest of the night—quit glancing over to see if my glass needed filling. Slowly the place started emptying out, some of the drinkers spilling through the dented steel door, others weaving up those dingy stairs behind the bar. When I showed no sign of leaving she came out from the bar and moved towards me like a tugboat ploughing up to the jetty.

"Last call was half an hour ago, pal. Time to clear out." Then, to a couple of men passed out near the back: "Wake up, fellas, and get the hell outta here."

"It's only midnight," I said, and she looked like she could mash my head against the table, standing there flicking her dull brown hair off her face.

"Jesus, girl," I almost said. And remembered it wasn't Martinello's, wasn't Georgie's old lady, Ev, playing bouncer.

"Rules, eh? If ya don't like it, go take a leak at Queen's Park." She licked her finger and drew it along one eyebrow, smudging the green paint around her eye, then put her hands on her bulky hips, staring at the beer on the table.

"You too young to have a taste for it or what? Huh? Your momma know where you are? Young fella like you don't belong in a place like this, you know." Then she laughed, a dry hacking laugh like I was some stupid, know-nothing kid lost his ma in the co-op store.

"Move it, mister. I got a streetcar to catch."

I pictured the room upstairs, nothing but a ragged sheet over the mattress.

"I could give ya a lift," I said, and she looked at me funny, like my fly was down or something.

"What? You got a car? Guys come in here wouldn't know where to put a key!"

"I'll drive ya home if ya want."

"What if I said you're fulla shit?"

Out back somebody started switching off lights, and through the yellow glare on the sidewalk I saw the streetcar glide past.

"Goddamn," she hissed, and somebody yelled, "Have a good one, Donna."

Then she turned to me, her face in a watery flash of neon from across the street. At least I wouldn't have to ask her name—in Blackett you already knew who everyone was.

"Where you parked?" she asked as we swung through the door, the rush of hot, sticky air like being ploughed in the face with a bowl of porridge.

"Over here," I said, side-stepping a puddle of something.

"Parliament and Queen?"

"I dunno."

She looked at me then like I had three heads.

"So what else don't you know, Newf? Aw, you coasters are all the same. Trawna's crawlin' with youse." She laughed, pushing her arms into the sleeves of her yellow sweater. Then she poked a cigarette between her lips, waiting for me to light it.

"So what brings you the hell up here?"

"Oh nothin' much. S'pose ya could say I'm just here on a toot." The sight of the Ford cheered me up, even made me feel hopeful.

"That's all you Newfs are in'erested in, havin' a good time. So how come I didn't have to scrape you off the floor tonight? Huh?"

"More to life than gettin' pissed," I said. Ma talking again.

"So you're up here for work, then."

"Yeah, yeah," I said. As if work was the ticket to heaven. I opened the door for her and she slid in.

"You got people up here, I s'pose."

"Naw," I said. "Don't know a soul. 'Cept for you."

"Okay," she said, watching the other cars. Then, pointing with her cigarette, she showed me the way to her place—way the hell on the other side of the city, it seemed—behind streetcars and cabs, a zillion other cars. Buildings all lit up as if nobody slept. I thought of Blackett, the empty black sky over it, quiet but for bursts of drunken laughter, beer bottles being smashed in the dirt outside Martinello's.

"It's a bugger the way things are so spread out," she said. "But you get used to it—took me a while too."

She was from some place in Saskatchewan, she said, as she led me up the narrow stairs to her flat—a room, really, with a kitchen sink and a hotplate, shared bath, squeezed like a rabbit-hole into the top of a tenement. The furniture looked new, like the stuff Ma sniffed at leafing through Sears' catalogue, flimsy and easy to move. Not the dark wooden stuff I'd grown up with, company-store issue bought on time when Ma and

Pa first set up house.

Next to the hotplate was a tiny chrome table with two chairs, the seats patterned like the Arborite. On the table was a nearly full bottle of Canadian Club.

"Takes a while to get on your feet," she said, kicking off her scuffed shoes. Then she wiped some glasses on a Kleenex, filled them with whisky and passed me one.

"To Trawna," she said, falling on the couch. She knocked hers back, leaned her head against the sunken cushions.

"Better'n moonshine," I said, the flash of fire on my tongue. I downed it, set the glass on the coffee table. It looked like a surfboard with wobbly screw-in legs.

"So what's your line, anyway?" she said, getting up to fetch the bottle. She still hadn't asked my name.

"Cars. I guess."

"What—you sell 'em or somethin'?"

I shrugged, smiled at her. She laughed again, a raspy sound like fingernails dragged across tarpaper, and stared into her whisky like there was dirt in it.

"So what the hell you doin' stayin' at the Nickel?" She splashed more whisky into my glass, then grabbed an orange towel off the radiator and disappeared into the dingy hall. I thought of Pa's suitcase waiting for me under that bed.

After a while she came back, all the warpaint scrubbed off, her face startling white under the ceiling light. It was like she'd been going through my thoughts with a poker.

"You can stay here. Just this once. You un'erstand? This ain't a revolving door."

I should've left it at that. But instead of grabbing a pillow and being happy just to pass out on the gold-coloured linoleum, I let the whisky start talking. I just wanted to pay her back. And without the makeup she wasn't bad-looking, either—she had light brown eyes and her body was so big and soft-looking in the fuzzy pink housecoat she'd put on. I helped her unfold the pull-out couch, already made up with sheets. When she flipped off the light and settled down on one side, still wearing her housecoat, I eased myself down beside her. Coils from the lumpy mattress digging in everywhere, like lying on a stony patch of ground. Then I leaned over on my elbow to kiss her, a quick peck that missed her sleepy mouth and caught her on the chin. She didn't flinch.

"Yer some nice," I tried, coaxing her towards me with one arm looped under her mousy hair. I knew she wasn't asleep. "How lucky can a fella get, meeting a girl like you his first night in the Big Smoke?" Never mind she was likely a good fifteen years older than me. I kissed her again, properly, and tried to slide the housecoat off her shoulders, but she grunted and rolled away.

"I wanna pay ya back for lettin' me stay."

"You will, one way or 'nother. It don't matter." Then she yawned, turning onto her side. I pawed at her shoulder another minute or two, since it didn't seem right to give up so easily. I didn't want to insult her. But something about the way she didn't seem to care if we did it or not took the wind out of my sails, the weariness of three days' worth of strange places putting me under at last.

*

It was around noon when I woke up, my head pounding like a flat tire flubbing the pavement. For a minute I didn't know where I was—thought for a second I was still behind the wheel.

"Get up, Jack," she snapped, her back to me as she slid into her underthings beneath the wrinkled housecoat, its fuzzy material stuck in the crack of her arse. "I got extra hours today an' I'm late aw'ready."

No question about me staying. Pain bursting behind my eyeballs, I jumped up, the metal legs of the bed banging against the floor. Fumbled for some word of thanks, some kind of apology—I wasn't sure what.

"When can I see ya again?" I asked, my hands pressed to my temples.

"You got to be kidding, right?" White sparks were flying around in my skull. "You're not serious?" she howled, doubled over, rolling up her pantyhose. When she looked up again her eyes were full of hate. "Some of us gotta earn a living, you know. Look. I don't owe you nothing. You get the hell outta here now." Her big hands flew up at her stringy hair, one of her big tits flopping out of her housecoat. She tucked it back in like it was a loaf of bread.

"I wantcha the hell out. Now."

She snapped up the venetian blind, the light like a pry-bar in my brain. For a second she stood there with her arms folded over her droopy middle—I could've been looking at Ma.

Then she grabbed her towel and ripped the chain-latch out of its groove, letting it bang against the doorframe as she took off to the john. From the hall nothing but muffled voices, the sound of a toilet running. I threw on my clothes, was just zipping up when she came in again, still wearing her robe but her hair combed, a splash of orange on her lips.

"Look, Donna, I'm a goner," I tried to joke, fumbling with the buttons on my shirt, stiff with old sweat, the stink of smoke and spilled rye. "Pullin' a fast one, see? Pullin' a Hank Snow, movin' on."

Not even stopping for a piss, I took the stairs two at a time, the sun like knives out on the sidewalk. Got into the Ford, dust so thick you couldn't see the plates. I'd forgotten to lock 'er, but everything was like I'd left it, nothing missing. I'll tell you, the roar of her engine turning over was like a tonic, even with the headache. And as I nosed her into traffic heading back east towards Yonge, I let myself get lost in the bright crawl of cars and stoplights till things started looking vaguely familiar.

As I turned north up Yonge, just a couple blocks shy of the Triple Nickel, I thought of Pa's suitcase, my clothes inside. I knew Ma would want to know what became of it, though she'd never ask. And in never asking she'd never have to know. So I kept driving north till I hit the 401, then headed east till the city was just a blur of burger joints and car lots. And I drove and I drove without stopping, putting three provinces behind me, till all I had left of two hundred bucks was a twenty and every nerve in my body was humming like the engine. Smells in the air told me I was getting closer, the whiff of dried mud and spruce giving way to salt and the sour stink of burnt coal.

*

"Where ya been, Arch?" Old Georgie looks up from the bar when I stagger in, fingers clawed from holding the wheel, buzz of the tires still spinning in my ears. He's all red in the face from bending over counting beer cases, big gut spilling over the top of his pants. Ev's there too, thumbing through bills from the cashbox. Smiles when she sees me, then shakes her head.

"Here we go," she mutters, rolling her eyes, a smoke dangling from her lips. I can't remember what day it is.

"B'ys down back want another round," Georgie barks and she reaches down for the bottles, loading them in her arms.

They're in the usual spot beside the shuffleboard, empty stubbies piling up in front of 'em. They hardly look when I sit down, like any night of the week. Like I never left.

"So Arch. How're t'ings up the g'rage?"

"Ain't seen ya 'round much last few times I been up there. See they got a new fella—"

"Hey, b'y, you been on the wagon or what? By Jaysus ya'd sooner see the bay freeze in August, now wouldn'tcha—"

Then they turn their heads and go on drinking.

I go up to the bar and ask Ev for a beer—the sour old thing, you can see the grey showing through that black mop. Georgie keeps stacking cases of Keith's. Guess it's a Saturday—he'd have some explaining to do if the Mounties ever saw this stash. Some kitchen party, they'd say, boys playing tarabish and drinkin' Seven-Up, saying their prayers for church next morning. Oh Lord. Martinello's Social Club—not like the Legion, where you got to join.

By the bar a tableful of miners and their old women are out for a night of it, the ladies in their stretchy pants and curls—*must* be Saturday night if they've bothered taking the rollers off—the kind of women Ma sees in the co-op store and just struts past, gripping her purse. They cackle to one another over the old guys' grumbling, drinking beer right from the bottle.

Ma would lock me out if she knew I came here. Tonight she'd probably die. She's always turned a blind eye to the drinking—but it'd be a different story if she knew I did it here. I always break out in a sweat helping her with the groceries in the co-op if one of those women is behind us in the lineup. They recognize me all right, but seeing who I'm with keeps them quiet. Yes, tonight it would kill Ma to know I'm here, and that I came here first, without stopping to tell her I'm home.

"Arch! Look out, wudja!" and darts start whizzing past my head for the board hanging lopsided by the bar. "Bull's eye!" grunts Georgie, ducking behind the Arborite as the old guys stagger up one by one to take their turns. "At least they're still standin'," he growls, pushing another Keith's at me, still capped. I open it on my buckle, though the rest of the guys in here use their teeth. Their goddamn teeth, all chipped off in front.

Then somebody starts retching and Georgie bustles out to give 'em the boot. "Do your business outside," he shouts, and Ev slithers over and shoves the guy out.

"I been to Toronto," I say when I sit down again, but the guys just nod, a bunch of bloody robots, and keep talking about layoffs and tonnage.

Finally one of them leans over, slurping beer, and says, "Didn't last long, didja?" They snicker into their bottles. "What brings you back so soon? Ya miss yer mama or what?"

"Women there are somethin'," I try, but they don't seem to hear, so I sit back and suck on my beer, listening to their stories, them stories you hear a million times where nothing really happens. But after a while I'm laughing and carrying on like the rest of them, the krick in my legs and the knot between my shoulders loosening up. Under the jumpy lights, Martinello's looks pretty good. Not as fancy as the Legion but beer's five cents cheaper. And there's pop bottles full of silver for sale out back if you want it.

Even Ev seems a little less sour after a couple of drinks. She's the business-minded one you see giving the boot to the rowdies, threatening to call the Mounties. A lot of bull, but better not to mess with her. Tonight she looks hot under all the makeup but I get an idea what Georgie sees in her, not afraid to call any guy's bluff.

"All right, b'ys," says one fella at our table, staggering up with his glass sloshing over. "To Georgie and Ev, and a valu'ble public service." The glass wobbles and half of it soaks me.

"Jesus, Arch, you take a leak or what?" and we all have a good laugh then, till Ev snarls, "Drink up, fellas. Let's get a move on." Next I know, her pointy toe's in my arse and we all roll out the door onto the dirt. A fine drizzle is falling, coating everything. Foghorns drone out past the cliff, the air all tarry with salt and the smell of dead leaves.

"How 'bout a lift over by the pit?" somebody says, and a notion comes into my head.

"Ain't goin' that way," I yell. I'm still not ready to go home—though I know Ma will be asleep.

"Take 'er cool, then, Arch," they say, and the bunch of them shuffle off in the dark, their wet heads gleaming under the telephone poles. They stagger a bit, shoving at one another as I turn the key in the ignition. Thank Christ she's still running, after that drive. The headlights swing through the fog and the rain starts to pelt the roof.

"Good fucking welcome home," I mutter to myself, reaching for the case under the seat. Extra-proof, from Quebec. Only one left. I drive down the main drag, empty as a war zone, and head out of town, not thinking much about where I'm headed. Pretty soon the granite gates come up on my left, and next thing I'm pulling in between the rows of gravestones, wheels up to the axles in mud. The cemetery hugs the edge of the cliff and in the dark I can see whitecaps, hear foghorns groaning louder. On a fine day the headstones look like bones perched up here, white marble worn nameless by wind and spray. Pa's buried here, and most of Ma's family, the ones who never made it up to Boston or New York, or Toronto.

The wheels spin in the mud, the Ford sinking in the ruts. It's pouring rain now—I keep the wipers on to see through the sheets of water sliding down the windshield. I climb out, ducking my ears under my collar, and try to heave her out. Just my luck the Mounties'll come along and want to know what the hell I'm doing, half-corked like this. Threaten to escort me home. Imagine the look on Ma's face this hour of the night, her hair down, clutching that old blue housecoat around her.

I put her in neutral and stand in the headlights, then heave with all my might, the car rocking like a baby in the churned-up ground. Then she chokes and sputters a bit, and dies altogether, the headlights cut like the beam of a lighthouse flashing in the wrong direction. I crawl back in and think about going to sleep, till the rain stops, at least. But instead I grab the last beer and stagger towards the nearest row of graves. My hair's plastered down, the sweat from it trickling into my eyes, but I'm too wet now to give a shit, stumbling over the lumpy ground towards the cliff, looking for Pa's plot.

I've only been there once before—the day they put him in it. Figure there can't be too many Thomas Gillises in here— not out at the edge. That's where he wanted to be, Ma insisted, though everybody knows the cliff is falling into the ocean, an inch or two each storm. *Put me near the bay*, Pa said, and that was that. Never mind if his bones wash out to sea someday, headstone and all. It's black granite, just his first name underneath "Gillis". *Room there for the rest of ya*, they joked down at the monument place. I haven't forgotten the look of the stone, its cold gloss, or that day in early spring, ground thawed just enough to dig the grave. Ma in her heavy black coat and Grace and me so solemn, usually a mouthy pair of kids. The others didn't make it home—couldn't get the time off work, they said, to come so far. They sent flowers, loads of flowers, and donations to the Cancer Society.

And now I stagger over rows of graves, bits of faded plastic poppies scattered over the dead grass. *MacDonald, Bonner, Martinello, MacNeil, MacKiggan, Boutilier, Dorey, McDonald, Macdonald, Dorey, Capstick, Gillis.* But no Thomas, no Thomas to be found anywhere. How long does it take the wind to rub off a name?

I don't give up, but wander in circles, the beer in my pocket rubbing against my hip. Water squelches up between my toes and the rain blows sideways like splinters of ice in my face, but I keep stumbling on, peering at the headstones, searching.

"Come on, you old bugger," I hear myself say. "Let me at least give ya a drink." I'm glad now of the rain and the dark, of how lonely it is out here on the cliff, though part of me wouldn't give a goddamn *who* was watching. "Where the hell are ya, you old bastard? Where the Jesus are ya?" And the ground seems to heave, the mud oozing up over my shoes, furrows between the graves sinking, awash in muddy water. When I look up again I see *Gillis* two stones away, and I lunge for it, sweaty tears pouring down my face. I see it's still not Pa, but I've had enough now. Biting the cap off the beer, I squat down and dump it out all over the soggy ground.

"Have one on me," I cry. "You old bastard. Wherever the hell ya are." And I fall between the headstones, watching the foam swirl away into the grass. Nothing left but a pale, pale scum.

The Driver

"At *your* age?" Hettie said when I called to tell her. "What if ya take a queer spell or somethin' behind the wheel?"

"Well," I said, "I just thought I should warn you. I didn't want you having a stroke first time you saw me driving past, tooting the horn."

"You'll never git yer licence, Irene."

What a mistake, telling her—I knew right away I shouldn't have mentioned it. *What, piano's not enough for ya? Why I've got enough work down here to keep me goin' till Doomsday, if you need somethin' to keep ya busy.* That would've been next, if I hadn't cut in.

"Thomas would've thought it was all right." I couldn't help myself.

"They don't hand out licences at the *drugstore*, ya know," she managed to squeeze in, before I could hang up. Always the last word, that woman. My poor brother—Lord only knows what he saw in her!

"Well, I've got business to attend to," I said, just as the line clicked. Business being a trip down to Northside, to Traders' car lot. You see, I had everything planned, right down to the colour. Red, shiny red, and big enough to ride in comfort. None of those foreign-made compacts for me, no Toyotas or Volkswagens. Something with four doors, solid. Big but not ostentatious, nothing so grand that my pupils and their parents would stop, gape-mouthed, on the sidewalk and slap their thighs. *It's that old doll, Miss Gillis. By the jeezus, don't tell me she's learnin' to drive after all these years.*

When I phoned Hettie I hoped she'd ask her young fellow, Arch, to give me a lift to Traders'. Or at least come with me on the bus and bring the vehicle back. Give him something to do, the layabout, and not all that young either, now that I think about it. Must be nearly twenty-eight, still living off his mama. Thomas would've died of embarrassment, if cancer hadn't taken him first. No, Arch hasn't worked a day in his life, unless you count pumping gas at the service station, and that, like everything else, just a flash in the pan. Takes after Hettie's crowd. Though I have to admit, for all her spinelessness, hers are good people. Harmless.

Salt of the earth, Thomas used to go on, enough to choke me at dinner-time when it was just the two of us here, after our parents passed on. I kept house and taught piano—good Lord, I must have had twenty students back then. Thomas had started right in as a foreman down at the pit. Above ground, of course—Papa wouldn't have stood for anything less.

Mama wasn't gone a week before Thomas started sneaking around with Hettie. A MacCallum, from down by the old coke ovens. He brought her home once for the Sunday roast. Never again, I told him. *Marry a MacCallum and you're done for.* Everyone in town knew how the men in that family carried on; one assumed the women could be no better.

But all the caution in the world wouldn't stop him. And before I knew it they were married, and a year after that the babies started coming. By then of course my brother was trapped. *Never mind.*

It's a red car I want. I saw it advertised in the *Post* last week: a 1969 Dodge Coronet, only three years old; clean, *lady-driven*. I know the kind they mean—four doors, nice wide seats front and rear. Lady-driven—no cigarette ash ground into the upholstery, or the clingy odour of stale smoke. Just the same, I plan to buy one of those paper pine trees to dangle from the rearview mirror. I love the smell of a brand-new vehicle, but that would be frivolous at this stage in life. No matter. I can see myself behind the wheel, my face lighting up the windshield. I can see the accessories I'll buy—a leather cover for the steering wheel, some soft plush seat-covers, perhaps. Once I've gotten myself on the road.

Seventy-three is too old to be learnin' to drive. What would Hettie know—never went further than the co-op store to get her groceries, material to make the kids' coats. "She's *decent*"— that's what I told Thomas I thought of her, after he'd finished carving up the rump roast and she'd gone off to fetch another plate. *Decent but clingy, the kind who likes attention.* Just look at what she's done to Arch—kept him home, held him back. If he were mine I'd have given him a swift kick. Her others, now, they've all managed to get away, even the girl. All but Arch.

"You're not going to hold me back," I told her when she heard I was going to Traders'. Tit for tat.

"It's got nothing to do with me," she said, chilly as March fog.

You know who not to call if you ever want to go somewhere, I almost said but didn't. It's not my nature to be petty. And chances are Hettie wouldn't go anywhere Arch couldn't take her, even if she were invited. Not even to the point and back, her favourite place on earth. Picturesque, I suppose. Though not the same since the province put in picnic tables and those log-cabin outhouses, and teenagers started loitering, roaring around on motorcycles and lying on the hoods of rusty cars in bathing suits and cut-off dungarees, practically naked. Hettie wouldn't see that, of course—too busy stooping to look at the bluets in the grass.

Thank the Lord I'm not like her. I had a career—still have one—two or three children after school every week. I don't intend to grow old by slowing down or having my traces tightened. Which is why a car is just the thing. *A car will keep me active.*

This is what I keep telling myself, as I stand at the bus-stop clutching my good white purse against my stomach. Kids race

—133—

past in cars with oversized tires, leaving behind tunnels of dust. My hat nearly comes off with one gritty gust, so I remove it, brushing dirt off the navy straw.

"Hey old woman don'tcha know church ain't till Sunday?" some young pup yells from a passing window, the radio blaring. I vaguely recognize the face—a former pupil perhaps. I turn and watch for my transportation, a schoolbus painted red and white, signal lights blinking like eyes. If only someone had offered a lift. But there it is: if a woman is to get anywhere, she must do it under her own steam. I've had a good deal of practice.

The driver slows, the car behind screeches its brakes, stops just in time. I climb up, gripping the warm metal railing, pulling my heavy body up the steps. It's uncommonly hot even for July, and I'm perspiring under my dress, the damp cotton clinging under my arms.

"Where ya goin'?" the driver wants to know, his eye following me like a cow's. The bus is empty, such a fine day and all. "Where dya wanta get off?" He chews a pink wad of gum, reaches up to scratch under his cap. The hair beneath is wet.

"Miss Gillis, ain't it? My sister useda take lessons from you." He eyes me in his mirror. "So where ya off to t'day?"

The liberties they take—as if everybody in Blackett believes the piano teacher is town property. *Old maid. Tom Gillis's old-maid sister.* I sit up straight, my purse on my lap, both hands pinching it shut.

"Traders', please. I would like to get out there."

"Oh yeah, I knows where ya mean. That car lot past the Gannon Road. I goes right by 'er. My sister, now, she don't go near the piano no more but she done right good for herself. Next time I talk to 'er I'll say I seen ya."

I force a smile, then stare out at the harbour flying past below the road, the edge of the cliff. Bouncing and jolting along on the hard leatherette seat I feel like a schoolgirl. *An automobile, my very own automobile.*

"What are ya up to at Traders'?" The cow-eye fixes on me

again in the mirror.

None of your beeswax, I feel like saying.

"I'm looking to purchase a vehicle."

"Well. Watch out for them salesmen—they can smell a lady driver a mile off." He laughs to himself, a sound like hiccoughs. He hugs the wheel with both arms, his shoulder-blades sharp folds in his blue polyester jacket.

"Some warm out," he says then. And I avoid the mirror the rest of the trip, past the docks, the Five-and-Ten and the fish plant. It gives me a little thrill seeing the gulls swarming over the wharfs, crooked and rotting, the oily green water. And the boats, rustbucket trawlers flying different flags: Russia, Spain, Portugal.

"Ain't much farther," the driver says, slowing up for the intersection where the Gannon Road cuts into Water Street. He jerks his head to the right, the skin on the back of his neck folding like a bulldog's. Just up ahead I see little red and blue streamers rippling like water in the breeze.

"Have a good one," he says, letting me out.

I'm a little out of breath by the time I reach the showroom. The sun is exceptionally strong and I fear I'm a trifle over-dressed, my dark cotton soaking up heat like a sponge. I should've worn something with short sleeves. But my arms— I don't like strangers seeing how they quiver when I write. And no doubt I'll be putting my John Henry on something this afternoon.

At the far end of the lot is my car, at least I believe it is. It's a lovely tomato-red, the price marked on the windshield in big yellow numbers. My throat tightens.

"Kin I help ya?" The salesman comes out of the office, stuffing his shirt-tail into the back of his pants, blinking at the brightness. His striped shirt has short sleeves and a beige stain on the pocket and he wears no tie. His pantlegs drag a little in the dust. Part of the lot is paved, the asphalt yellow-grey under all the black tires. The rest is packed dirt, with dusty potholes and dandelions springing up.

"I'm here to see the car."

"Now which one didja have in mind?"

"The red one." I hold my purse to my chest.

"Oh yeah, the Dodge. Can't go wrong wit' her." He walks me over to the car, his thin lips curling at the corners. "Check 'er out." He opens the driver's side. The interior is the colour of beets. Then he reaches in and pulls something, popping open the hood. "New transmission. She should last ya a good long while."

I glance down at my white sandals, gritty dust between my stockinged toes. I would rather not look under the hood, all those tubes and plugs and tanks—*too much like a person's innards*. It's not important to me how it works. Like my Heintzman—I don't need to see inside to hear the notes.

"Git in if ya want," the man says, tapping his foot, his thumbs hooked through his belt-loops. I slide behind the wheel, my knees squeezed together, holding my skirt to keep it from twisting. "Thirty-five hun'red and she's yours." I notice a little tear in the vinyl seat, greasy fingerprints on the dashboard.

"I'd need five hun'red down. What ya pay a month's up to the bank—I s'pose you've talked to them." He looks at his watch, black against his freckled skin.

"I prefer to pay cash." His eyes are like gasoline on water. They drop to my purse.

"Suit yerself. But ya better try 'er out first. Lemme grab the keys."

"But I don't drive."

"Aw! So ya don't want 'er for yerself."

"I take my test next week," I lie. He scratches behind his ear and little white flakes sift over his collar.

"I'll get the keys and take ya for a spin then. How's that?"

The engine roars as he turns the key and pushes the pedals. Then the car jerks into gear and we creep forward, bumping up and down till we reach the pavement. He signals, then pulls out into the empty street.

"Good day for the beach," he says, nosing up to a stop sign. "See? She runs like a dream."

"That's far enough," I say, "It seems like a very nice car." He smirks up at the rearview.

Back in the cluttered little office he rummages through the desk. An ashtray spills over with cigarette ends, some smudged with garish shades of pink. He goes to a dusty filing cabinet and pulls out some papers for me to sign. I open my purse and take out the bills, crisp and brilliant, held together with an elastic—exactly as the bank passed them to me this morning. He watches my hands counting them out. His eyes light on my emerald, as if he can see it sparkling under the smudges on it. I finish counting and he relieves me of the bills, flipping through them like a hand of tarabish, his lips moving slightly, cigarette bobbing up and down.

"Beauteeeful," he says.

"One slight problem," I say delicately.

"No sweat, eh?" he says, grabbing his greasy-looking jacket from a chair. "Since it's so slack, and yer payin' cash, I'll do a free delivery."

"I'm much obliged," I say, getting in the passenger side.

*

It's not as if I don't know *how* to drive. Thomas taught me, before he got mixed up with Hettie. After dinner Sundays we'd go out in the yard and sit in his roadster, and practise putting it in gear. Pressing the accelerator, letting out the clutch *ever so slightly*. Like nudging a stodgy pupil towards completing a piece, halting and painful, with many bumps and starts at first, stalling. But easier, smoother with practice. Thomas was a patient teacher; by the time he began courting Hettie I was quite confident on the road.

One day the three of us took a drive out to the point to look for lady's slippers, and Thomas let me take the wheel there and back. Without mishap, in spite of some distraction—

Hettie's remark about the flowers' scent, how they smelled like one's fingers after changing a diaper. Good Lord, Thomas should have guessed then what he was in for; those MacCallums are well known for their breeding. And I do *not* mean pedigree. But marry they did, going forth to breed like cats, and that was the end of my driving career. Who knows what became of the Model T?—probably, like everything else of Thomas's, it got sucked into that bottomless hole of raising children and *her* needs. I suspect when the Depression came he sold it to buy coal.

But how much can one forget—especially one so quick of mind and nimble of touch as myself? I have no more trouble playing a Bach invention, without the music, than when I was a girl. Which is why I've done so well with my pupils over the years.

But haven't you ever missed having children of your own? Hettie has asked on more than one occasion, most recently a church tea with half the ladies' auxiliary listening, teacups poised mid-air, lips pursed.

Can't you hear? They are like my own. What better creation than a nurtured talent, the pleasure on a youngster's face after he or she has run through a piece flawlessly? Of course, I've never stooped to respond.

But I know I can drive. And this new vehicle is automatic, which they say removes the stress. All I need is a little practice, out to the point and back a few times early in the day, before the young people are out speeding.

I have my beginners'. Nobody blinked when I walked into the Motor Vehicles office at Blackett town hall. It was one of my old pupils who waited on me, got me to take the little written test. Questions and answers, true or false, with and without my glasses on. I passed with flying colours—the clerk said I probably could have done it without my glasses. That was a month ago. It says I have sixty days to take my driver's test and get the real thing.

So there. Already I can see myself steering the Dodge along

Main Street, past the co-op and the bench outside the Legion where the old fellows sit, day in and day out, smoking cigarettes and spitting on the sidewalk. Heck, once I've gotten acclimatized I might go as far as the new mall in Northside. I hear they're building a supermarket there.

*

The first morning I wake with the birds and dress quickly—slacks, for comfort. I skip my usual breakfast of toast and tea and slip outside. It can't be past six-thirty, for the neighbours aren't up. The entire street seems to be asleep. On the little patch of grass between the sidewalk and the veranda, a robin roots out a worm. Everything glistens, the sky a perfect blue.

The car sits beside the house, halfway up the wide, level drive of crushed limestone. There's plenty of space between the house and the neighbours' delphiniums, a broad border of grass between the drive and the veranda. No danger, then, of scraping the shingles or bumping the steps. I know of a woman—someone Hettie chums with at church—who backed her daughter's car right into the porch. *Hettie never learned to drive.*

The man from the car lot wanted to park it in the barn for me, but I told him, *It's all right, my brother's boy is coming over to give me a driving lesson later.* Truth is, I was a little nervous about starting off in reverse and having to manoeuvre through the barn door. It would be such a shame to mar the paint, my first try.

I unlock it and get in, my head high, as if this is something I've done a thousand times. I put in the key and turn it, hold it a trifle too long, causing the engine to bark. I tap the accelerator quickly, as if it's a spider, then tug the gearshift into neutral.

The car rolls forward a little and I stamp on the brake, giving myself a jolt. *This must be what they mean by whiplash,* I think. But the engine keeps purring, purring, and once I catch my breath I hold the brake and tug the gearshift down to drive.

Ever so slowly I let the brake off, allowing the car to creep forward. *One foot. Stop. Another foot. Stop. Another foot. Stop.* And so on, until the front bumper nearly touches the barn doors.

I can see Ina Fraser at the screen next door, in her nightdress and her hairnet. I tootle the horn, louder than I intended, and she disappears. I think of Thomas sitting in the driver's seat in the Model T, showing me the gears with the motor off, the clutch in. I decide to try reverse.

You are not going to hit the barn, I tell myself, holding my breath as I press the brake and find the gear. I swear the birds have stopped singing. I look down at my feet, check that they're on the right pedals, gently nudge the gas. A slight jerk and I'm moving backwards—flying backwards, actually—out the driveway, over the sidewalk, darting across the street like wildfire. It's not until I reach the opposite sidewalk that I remember to hit the brake.

The car comes to rest on the MacDonalds' lawn, inches from their hawthorn. Ina Fraser comes dashing out into the street, cupping her hands around her eyes to peer through the windshield.

"Mother of God," she says, shaking. "You might've been killed, Irene."

When I'm able, I push down on the door handle and stumble out onto the grass, my stomach still in my throat. By which time Mr. MacDonald has come out and is ducking down beside the fenders, surveying the damage to his lawn.

"Lucky thing there was nothin' comin'," he says, blowing into his hand. He looks down at the ruts under the tires, and starts to laugh. "Mind if I park 'er someplace else?" I wait for a crack about lady drivers, but he simply gets in and, racing the motor, backs out to the street, one arm along the top of the seat. Ina Fraser lays her gnarled hand on my wrist. "There there," she says. She's forgotten about the hairnet.

"It seemed to get away from me," I say, staring at her pink curlers. "Now if you'll excuse me."

Mr. MacDonald backs the car into my yard, as far as it can go.

"Ya might get yer nephew over to take you out. Be yer *shofer*," he says.

"That won't be necessary." I smile sweetly, waiting for him to cross the street before I get back in. And for a good hour I practise inching backwards and forwards, until my stomach starts to rumble. Then I lock it up and go inside for breakfast, feeling rather pleased with myself.

*

I practise like this every morning for a week, rising at dawn to go outside and sit in the Dodge. At first I worry about disturbing the neighbours, particularly Ina, but my fears are soon allayed. It's such a quiet car when one knows how to handle it. Far quieter than some pupils I've had, whose sour notes would raise the dead. Though in forty years Ina has never complained— I'll give her that. But what I cannot *abide* is her trepidation: Ina is jumpy as a garter snake.

"*Don'tcha think ya might have Hettie's fella come up an' show ya the ropes?*" she has the gall to holler today while letting in the cat. I've had the Dodge exactly seven days now and haven't heard a word yet from Hettie or her *excuse* for a son.

"If ever there was one needed to be shown a few things," I mutter back. Likely Ina hears it, too, though perhaps not. She can be hard of hearing.

Knowing she's watching, likely from her kitchen window, I go to the barn and open the double doors, propping them wide with the boards Thomas always used. Once they are secure, I get back in the car, put it in reverse and manoeuvre it into the barn flawlessly, just enough space between the fenders and Papa's workbench to open the door and squeeze out. *There you go, Ina.*

After Thomas left, I stopped going into the barn. It still smells of grease and sawdust, Papa's well-oiled tools—a pleasant surprise. Along the walls, nailed to the wooden framing, are Papa's licence plates, old ones in odd combinations of colour. Blue and white, like the high school's colours. Black and yellow, the colours of the university where I would have studied music if not for the war.

I glance at the Dodge and remember it hasn't any plates. These will come once I've passed the big test—in plenty of time. That's enough for today, I think, letting the wooden doors swing shut. The sun makes me dizzy after the musty gloom of the barn. But looking up I see it's still early, and neither a cloud nor a hint of fog in sight. A lovely time to visit the point, unspoiled by reckless teenagers and whining, sunburnt children.

Yes, I know it's illegal to drive without a proper licence. But in the back of my mind stirs a picture of Thomas and me drinking lemonade on a cloth spread between the spruce trees, and nothing before us but the wide flat ocean, pale blue with silver currents snaking off to the horizon, the quiet thrum of bluebottles in the boughs above us.

Just this once. I won't do it again. Nobody will know the difference. Just this once.

I go inside to change into a skirt, then find my clip-on sunglasses on top of the piano, using the front of my blouse to wipe off the dust. A thick film has also gathered on the burled veneer, but there isn't time to fuss, so I drop the curved cover over the keys. I go to the buffet where I keep my purse and then to the porch for my straw bonnet.

Hastily I open up the barn and get into the car, rolling the window down an inch and making sure all the doors are locked. It starts like a charm and I creep ahead, down the length of the drive, stopping at the sidewalk. A car races past, a woman with small children in the back. From the other direction comes a pickup truck, the driver wearing a ballcap. I flip down the dark lenses on my spectacles, then look both ways. Then ever so slowly I pull out into the street, like a boat leaving dock.

Thank goodness for my height—I have no trouble seeing

over the wheel. It always embarrasses me to see elderly people driving, shrunken down in the seat, their little white heads barely visible above the dashboard. I come to a halt at the stop sign where Chestnut meets Main, then click on the signal. Left. Nothing in sight, so I make my turn and continue along Main, a full five miles below the speed limit.

The traffic is a little heavier than I'd expected—bread must be on two-for-a-dollar at the co-op. But I stop and start, stop and start, apace with the other drivers, some of whom slow down and honk at the fellows in front of the Legion or the people lined up waiting for the bank to open. I continue to float along, following the flow of traffic past the town hall, the liquor commission, the church, then on towards Mac-Kiggan's garage. The fellow in front of me stops and rolls down his window and shouts to somebody at the gas pumps, and without thinking I swing around to see who it is. Hughie Capstick, the town policeman, leaning out the window of his bright blue cruiser. My heart contracts when I remember about the plates. But he shouts something back to the driver ahead, who laughs loudly and squeals off. Pressing the gas, I hold my breath, my eyes on the rearview. Half a block ahead, in front of the co-op store, I have a second to glance back. Hughie hasn't moved, his head still hanging out the window. Another block and I've made it to Pond Street, and the traffic has thinned out completely. There I make a right and start to breathe easier, my foot a little lighter on the pedals.

I follow the pavement along the marsh, willing myself not to glance at the cattails growing up to the shoulder. I pass a cluster of mobile homes, some with large tires on the roofs. To pin them down in a gale, I suppose. Others with the bodies of rusted cars in their yards, the bright colours of children's toys scattered here and there. Then I come to a cluster of old shingled buildings, the tall white storefront of a general store, boarded up and sprayed with names and disgusting words. *Darrell—Darleen, Darleen loves Darrell. —you. Jesus Saves.* Good God, I think, if only the parents of these children would try interesting them in something. Music, for instance.

Just past the general store I slow down to watch for the dirt road that leads to the point. Even at a crawl I nearly miss it, and have to back up a little to make the turn. The road is rough and full of potholes shiny with wet mud. The noise of stones flying up into the undercarriage puts me on edge, like the sound of teeth breaking, or gunshots. So I'm quite relieved when I pass the last trailer and the road narrows into a muddy track, a bright strip of grass up the middle. The car skims along, huckleberry bushes ticking the fenders like fast writing on a chalkboard.

At last I reach the cliff, where the road peters into a sandy path through the dunes, the beach on one side, a brackish pond behind. I sit for a moment with the engine running, looking out at the gulf. On the horizon a thread of fog gathers, greyish clouds thickening over the water. The wind has picked up and little whitecaps ruffle the surface, a dull blue-grey as far as the eye can see. To the left the land seems to drop off into the water, below the tangled brink of wild rose and blueberry. At the far end of the beach the point extends out into the bay like a slice of cake. The rocks are a greyish sandstone etched with black, the beach the same shade, dotted with shore coal.

I turn off the car and step out, my white cardigan draped around me like a shawl. The sun has gone behind a cloud, the wind has the bite of rain in it, and I slip my arms into the sweater, clasping it tightly at the neck. I move back a little out of the wind, and step in something pink and gooey, somebody's old chewing gum. It sticks to the sole of my sandal, hardening in the chilly air. I wish the sun would come back, I think disgustedly. Under bright sun the rocks sparkle—like the sugar on gingersnaps, I used to think when I was a child.

I try scraping my shoe on a clump of marram, then look around for a stick or perhaps something the tide has washed up—an old stave from a lobster-pot, a piece of tree-root polished smooth. The ground is littered with chip bags and candy wrappers, a man's old black rubber in the bushes. Down on the beach I find more junk, worn Javex bottles and pieces of rope, a shoe. Never a pair; always just one.

I hear a car and glance up towards the Dodge. A familiar-looking green car is pulling in beside it. Then who gets out but Arch and his mother. He goes around to her side and helps her with something—buckets or pails, it looks like. He takes them from her and walks behind as she starts poking along the edge of the cliff, head bent in the wind. I watch as she stoops down, and squats. Picking something—blueberries—it's too late for raspberries. Though Lord knows that woman would be out here regardless, so long as there was something going for nothing.

I watch till they're just two black sticks on the cliff, one rather tall and gangly, the other no bigger than a minute. Once they've disappeared behind the spruces, I struggle back up to the car, the dirty sand filling my shoes. I start the car, not bothering to let it warm up, tugging this way and that to get it turned around. Without a glance I gun the engine, bouncing over the ruts like mad until I'm back in civilization. If you consider mobile homes civilized. Eyesores, actually. But I'm quite relieved to see them now, dogs and children and beat-up swing-sets, rows of laundry flapping.

So relieved that I forget the stop sign just before the general store, where the dirt road meets pavement. Or more precisely, I don't see it, it blends in so well with the rust-red building opposite the store.

Just as the tires touch asphalt, a milk truck comes barrelling from nowhere, the horn one long blare, the blood-thinning screech of brakes. I shut my eyes and stamp on the brake, waiting for the crush of metal, of shattering glass. But miraculously it doesn't come, and when I open my eyes the milk truck is gone. My car is splayed across the road, the motor still purring.

And then I see the blue cruiser creep out of the boarded-up gas station across the road, barely stirring the dust. It pulls up beside me, Hughie's ruddy face filling the window.

"Don'tcha know you're *contravening* the Motor Vehicles

Act, drivin' without *registration*? Lemme see yer licence."

"But don't you recognize me, Hughie? I gave you lessons one winter. You were eight, I think. But then you caught the mumps and stopped coming. Yes, that was it. You must remember me."

"Git yer car off the road, then I wanta see yer licence."

"You loved to sight-read, don't you remember? You were very good at it—"

"Move yer car, I said."

My hands are shaking so hard I can barely grip the wheel. My mind goes blank, and for a second I can't think what to push. Hughie stands there, his knuckles on his holster, whistling through his teeth. I fumble for the gearshift and the car gurgles, lunging forward before it stalls.

"Move over," Hughie growls, and I slide to the passenger side, trembling so hard I can barely fix my skirt, hitched up to my knees, the lace from my slip showing.

He starts up the car and pulls over in front of the ruined storefront.

"Licence, *please.*"

I feel the tears springing just as rain starts to spatter the windshield, loud as bird droppings. I open my bag, remove the little black change purse, a package of tissues.

"I—I seem to have misplaced it," I say, turned to the window so he won't see my face. And just as I turn, putting my hand over my mouth, a green car pulls around the corner. Arch and Hettie. They slow down and gawk when they see the police car, Hettie's neat white head swivelling to and fro to get a good look. I cover my face with my hands. Too late. Even at this distance I can see her eyes grow wider, her neck a little longer. She says something to Arch, who jams on the brakes and starts pulling over.

"Kin I see yer insurance then?" Hughie is saying impatiently.

I barely hear, I'm so intent on waiting for them to park and waltz over, the two of them demanding to know what's going on.

"I'm gonna hafta book ya, missus. Whatcha been doin' is a serious *offence*."

But then they do a strange thing. I see Hettie nudging Arch and him shaking his head, and next thing they pull back onto the pavement and drive off. Just like that, Hettie looking straight ahead as if she's seen a ghost, or worse. Without so much as glancing back.

"What if ya *kilt* somebody, huh? Look, missus, I'm doin' ya a *favour*, haulin' ya in like this. Inta the cruiser now."

"But my car—?"

"We'll 'ave 'er towed. Then I'd suggest ya put 'er in storage till ya get yer papers."

"I see."

"Meantime you kin expec' one *helluva* fine."

"Yes."

"And one bitchuva time findin' someone to *insure* ya. That is, if yer *lucky* enough to git yer licence."

I dab my eyes with a tissue. The rain is streaming down the windshield now, like inside a waterfall.

"I'm *warnin'* ya now," he says, playing with the wipers. "If it was me I'd try sellin' 'er and gittin' my money back." He switches them off, letting the windshield blur. And just before he pulls out the key: "Nice day for ducks, ain't it, *Miss Gillis*?"

The Pink Teacup

April 1983. There's something about the sky after it rains, the soft grey clouds moving over the potholes, the telephone poles like crooked crosses up and down Atlantic Street. It makes me think my grandmother is up there watching. Though of course I know she isn't, and nothing will bring her back. You see, I still can't grasp that she's gone, though she's been dead nearly two months—it will be two months next week. Twice now I thought I'd seen her, once coming out of Woolworth's, another time by the bakery. Everything reminds me of her: the teacup I keep on my dresser, also the smell of carbolic soap, which she used to scrub the kitchen floor. See, I think of Hettie all the time, she's always there in the space between my thoughts. These things are just reminders.

My uncle says some things you don't get over, you just get used to. Maybe it's true. But one thing I'll never get used to is how long my mother waited to take me to my grandmother— I'll never understand why she didn't do it sooner. Not that I didn't have a good long time with Hettie, it's just that now she's gone it hardly seems long enough. Some days I wish my mother had taken me to her the day I was born. It would've been better that way—then maybe Hettie wouldn't have seemed so worn out, so *used up*, that first time my mother took me home to her.

*

June 1973. We left Halifax the same day school closed. My mother had saved up all year for the trip, in a coffee jar on top of the fridge. She kept the two of us with odd jobs, cleaning doctors' homes in the south end. She always seemed tired, and it used to irk me to come home from school and find her snoozing on the pull-out bed.

The train took all night, but finally started slowing down near the shore. The sea was bright blue, nothing like the grey harbour I was used to. My mother stubbed out her cigarette and closed her eyes as we passed rows of houses, some muddy shades of brown and red, others just silvery shingles. You could see the spread of the town, places like toy blocks scattered on a sooty carpet, not a tree in sight and the ground black as tar. Out past the bay were mountains, cliffs jutting into the water.

"What's that?" I demanded as we passed the pit yard, pointing at the rusty metal buildings, the pulleys and cables.

"Nothing you need worry about," my mother said, picking pearl varnish off her thumbnail. Everything looked so *raw*— not what I was used to, coming from a city where the streets were paved and people worked in office buildings, doing clean jobs. *(With their heads, not their hands,* as my mother put it.)

"Where are we?" I kept asking, even as the brakes started hissing. She stared out the window, squeezing the strap of her dirty white purse.

"I've told you a million times already," she said, yawning into the mirror of her compact.

I just wanted it pinpointed, put on the map somehow, though she had spelled out "Blackett" for me, even written it backwards on the motion-sickness bag the conductor passed us.

"Maybe we'll get you something new to wear," she sighed, rubbing at a stain on my pedal-pushers. "That is, if you can find anything worth buying here." The way she said it made me feel we were going to the end of the earth, as the train shuddered up to the platform.

My mother didn't seem to mind that there was nobody to

meet us, but then we were used to being alone. And I was in no rush to see my grandmother, since nothing I'd heard made me anxious to meet her. More and more I was feeling like an extra bag best left on the train.

"How will we find it?" I asked, as if the town was as strange to my mother as it was to me.

"It's not that big a place," she hissed, hopping over the switch-tracks, the suitcase bumping against her thigh and me trudging along behind. I kept looking up and down for trains.

"It's not exactly Grand Central—next one's not due till eleven." I wondered how she could be so sure.

It wasn't far to my grandmother's—her garden gate was just behind the red brick station, half hidden in weeds and overgrown grass. My mother yanked open the gate and pulled me into the yard, past some tiny beet greens pushing through the oily dirt.

"Try looking pretty for Ma," she whispered, raking her fingers through my ponytail as we crossed the yard. Being eight, I didn't much care how I looked, to my grandmother or anybody else. Though I was bothered by the dribble of dried spittle near my mother's lip as we went up to the door. The air was murky and sweet—the smell of coal, I soon learned, which seemed to seep from the ground and hover in the clouds.

My mother tapped at the screen door and after a minute a tiny hunched woman in a yellow apron appeared, scowling as if we'd caught her at a bad time. But when she saw who it was she wiped dough off her hands and opened the door. At first she didn't see me; I was cowering behind my mother, not even sure this *was* my grandmother. Wiping her fingers on her apron, she gripped my mother's arm to hold her still and kiss her cheek, as if she were a butterfly that might flutter off any second. "Grace, Grace," she kept murmuring, my mother rolling her eyes at me over Hettie's humped shoulder, waiting for her to stop.

"This is my girl, Ma," my mother explained, twisting the adjustable pearl ring on her finger. Without smiling or speaking

Hettie bent down and touched my cheek with her finger, dry and scratchy as dead leaves. I shrank back from her wrinkled face, the soft white hairs around her mouth, her smell of flour and soap. I felt vaguely ashamed.

Your grandma had lovely skin before she got married was about all my mother had told me—aside from the fact Hettie had *chosen poorly* and *worn herself out* cooking and cleaning for my grandfather. I knew, too, that my mother had eight brothers. But at my age this seemed unremarkable, neither good nor bad, pleasant nor disastrous. I was an only child. Hettie had seen me once when I was still in diapers but I had no recollection of that one visit.

"So this is Nancy," she finally said, turning away to let us in. I had been expecting more—not exactly to be treated like my scuffed sneakers were glass slippers, but at least to be given a hug.

"Come in, come in." She herded us into the steamy kitchen, fussing around the big stove, lifting lids and stirring as if to make up for the time spent greeting us. "Would you look who's here, Arch," she called to a large man behind a newspaper, rocking idly back and forth beside the stove. My mother's brother, I guessed, the one who couldn't hold a job. He put down the paper and stood up stiffly, hitching up his workpants and doing up the top button of his flannel shirt.

"Well, look what the cat's drug in," he muttered, pumping my mother's hand a few times, then settling back in the rocker. Hettie fluttered around the room, scooping coal from a bucket in the corner and dumping it on the fire. Then she went over and straightened the white lace curtains, swiping at their soot-smudged hems with a corner of her apron.

"Are you expecting someone?" my mother asked dully, as if the fuss was for somebody else.

"Of course not," Hettie sniffed and poked at the fire. "Dinner at noon, supper at five, even though it's just Arch and me." She seemed offended that anyone would need reminding.

On the train my mother had whispered, almost as if talking

to herself, that Hettie had been a widow for eighteen years now, as though it was something that mattered. About my uncle she'd confided almost nothing; I only knew what I'd heard her telling her friend Ina once when she was over fixing my mother's hair, the smelly stuff from the Toni box spilled on the kitchen table. Arch eyed me now without interest.

"Where'd you find the kid?" he sneered at my mother, his idea of a joke.

"So how's work at the Princess?" she sneered back, and I remembered Ina snickering when my mother said he'd lasted a day at the mine, *above ground at that*, before getting sacked.

Hettie was rummaging around the pantry for extra plates but you knew she could hear everything. "You heard Arch got laid off," she called in a pinched voice—for my benefit, though it was aimed at my mother. As Arch shuffled to the sink to rinse his hands, I remembered her telling Ina after a few beers that her brother hadn't worked since 1970, and I waited for her to remind him. But then Hettie bustled in, setting some plates on the yellow table, the cutlery in a tall glass.

All through her stew my mother kept her head down as if she were ducking raindrops, even when the clock on the wall started chiming out noon. Somewhere down the tracks a whistle blew and she smirked into her spoonful of turnip. "Still the same old grind," she sighed.

"Somethin' wrong with that?" Arch jerked his chair back on the leaf-patterned linoleum.

"Stop it!" Hettie cried, then turned to me. "Never mind," she said, "never mind." But by now I was longing for our little flat in the city, even the safety of the train. My mother lit a cigarette and flipped ashes into her saucer, ignoring Hettie's glare.

Afterwards, while my mother washed up, my grandmother led me to a room in the attic, climbing the narrow painted stairs with her palm pressed against the bumpy wallpaper. "This was your mother's room," she said, leaning in the doorway. I hung back, waiting for her to go in first. "You can share the bed. I'm sure yer used to doubling up," she added, tucking her hands inside the apron.

"Grandmother," I started to say, but she pulled the crooked door tight, as if to shut me in with my mother's past. Her *old* life, before she met my father.

Hettie had meant for me to nap—she said I must be worn out from the train-ride—but I was too wound up to sleep, and the iron bed too lumpy. From a nail hung a man's clothes, moth-eaten wool trousers and a grey wool cap. My grandfather's things, my mother later explained. I went to the yellow dresser and pulled open the drawers. I don't know what I was looking for—nothing special, just some clues to what my mother might have been like growing up. There was nothing but a chocolate box full of beach glass, pebbles of mauve and midnight blue, the colour of Noxzema jars, and some blank yellowed paper. After a while the musty heat made me sleepy, and I dozed the rest of the afternoon.

*

For supper there was sliced tomato and Hettie's johnnycake with tinned meat, slabs of it pink and spongy as a tongue, the kind with a key to open it. The key made me think there must be some delicious surprise inside, but the taste made me gag. Again my mother insisted on doing the cleaning up. After the dishes were put away, we all went outside and got into Arch's big green car. Hettie sat up front with him, my mother and I in back. For a while we followed the train tracks, then started heading towards the mountains. Nobody talked much until we reached the edge of town, where the earth seemed to change from black to green.

"Nice evenin'," Arch said to my grandmother, as if there were nobody in the back seat.

"Lovely," Hettie agreed. "And not even the first of July yet." The braids she wore twisted around her head were starting to unravel from the day's work; her gnarled fingers twitched at the loose strands.

"Which way, Ma?" said Arch when the pavement ended. Though they both seemed to know where we were going, as if it were somewhere they could have found with their eyes closed.

"The old MacIsaac place, Archie, at the foot of the hill."

My mother gazed sullenly out the rolled-down window, bored, I suppose, by the meadows and tumbled-down barns and houses, the purple choke-weed growing in the ditches. I'd have been bored too if not for the newness of it, the strange thrill of riding in my uncle's car with my grandmother.

"You go for drives every night?" my mother asked, watching fence-posts zip past. Dust was flying in the window, and the smell of hay and manure.

"Only when it's fine," Hettie said, as if she needed reminding about the island's weather. *Drift ice in the bay till June.*

"Yeah," said my mother, staring at my sneakers, refusing to smile.

Arch pulled up beside a field overgrown with spruce trees. He stayed behind the wheel smoking while the rest of us got out and I started wading through the grass, daisies and devil's paintbrush up to my knees. Hettie pointed the flowers out to me, one by one, giving them each a name.

"Weeds," said my mother, leaning against a boulder by the ditch. She took her cigarettes from her purse but seemed in no hurry to light one. Hettie was moving purposefully through the grass now; reluctantly my mother got up and started following.

"Her knees are bad," she whispered as Hettie knelt down to pick something. Strawberries, wild strawberries. I had never seen such tiny berries, and I fell into the grass beside her, my greedy fingers grabbing them stems and all.

"This always was the spot," said Hettie, a speck of red juice on her shrivelled lip. "I used to bring the whole crowd picking when your mother was still a baby, after Sunday school. Them days we'd walk all the way out here and back."

Arch craned out the window, glaring at my mother to start bringing Hettie back to the car. But she didn't notice, she was standing apart from my grandmother and me, watching something in the trees.

"Makes a lovely pie." Hettie smiled, struggling to her feet. "If only we'd brought a pail." And I thought, *Oh yes, next time.* "Already past their best," she muttered, grappling for my mother's arm and letting herself be led to the road. I realized then it was unlikely we'd come back. Hettie held out her handful of berries to Arch, who looked away into the rearview mirror and twigged the car into reverse. This didn't seem to bother her.

"Let's have a cone," she said brightly. "My treat." And something seemed to let go a bit then, like shoelaces being loosened. My mother smiled at me and by the time we reached the paved road we were chanting, *I scream, you scream,* all the way to the crossroads dairy. My mother and I chose strawberry, savouring the sticky trickle down our chins, over our wrists. Hettie wagged her head at us, her long white braids all coming unpinned, and took quick bites of vanilla, careful not to get it on her dress. Arch, who preferred to smoke, steered home with one hand.

*

When I woke the next morning the sheets beside me were cold and smooth, no sign at all that someone had slept there. I noticed my mother's purse gone off the dresser, her clunky white shoes missing too. There was a noise outside the door—where my clothes now hung, my grandfather's having been removed—and as I lay there, staring at the cracks in the ceiling, Hettie came in and stood by the bed. Her hair was tangled and loose, as if she hadn't had time to put it up. I was startled by its length, spiky and kinked from the braids, and how like a child it made her look, a small, shrunken child.

"I think ya should know, Nancy," she said in a rough

whisper, trying to be gentle. "Yer mother has business back home." First I thought she was saying, *Get up, your mother's leaving. Don't keep her waiting.* But there was no urgency, Hettie settling stiffly on the edge of the bed, tracing something on the quilt with her thumb. Slowly she eased her legs up, one after the other, and I stared at the bunions wearing through her slippers. She lay back on my mother's pillow, hands folded on her sagging bosom, staring, too, at the cracked plaster.

"Yer mother's gone back to Halifax," she explained, picking her words. "Yer to stay here for a while, till she sorts things out." She sighed, leaning close enough to touch her lips to my forehead. She seemed old as stone, though I thought I'd heard my mother say she wasn't quite seventy.

"Come down now and have some breakfast—" she began, groaning a little as she got up from the bed.

"She *can't* leave me," I cried, staring. She looked so small and white, standing there wringing her hands, the knuckles showing through the skin. "My mother *wouldn't* leave—" I pushed my face into the pillow, kept swallowing to stop the tightness in my throat.

"Shhh, now," she said over and over, as I dragged the quilt over my head and let the tears soak the pillow. Just wanting her to go away, take back what she'd said. But she wouldn't leave, even after I stopped crying. I could feel her standing there, holding my pink housecoat, waiting.

"It ain't the end of the world, child," she finally said. Though from her sighs I figured it had to be, even when she pulled back the covers and wiped my cheek with her hand. She helped me into my housecoat and pulled a Kleenex from her sleeve, dabbing at my face. Then she led me downstairs by the hand, firmly, as if expecting me to try to escape.

" . . . thought my child-raisin' days were *done*," she muttered under her breath.

In the kitchen Arch turned to the sink, fishing his teeth from a glass. "Like a goddamn stray dumping its litter," he said, not looking at either of us.

"Archie!" Hettie burst.

Before he could answer I turned and dashed back up to bed, sliding under the covers. I waited for someone to come, for Hettie's uneven footsteps on the landing. But nobody did and after a while I got up and put on my clothes. (My mother had placed everything neatly in the dresser; she must have done it while I slept.) Then I knelt by the window, flies hitting the panes, and stared for a long time at the rooftops down the street, backyards like a crossword puzzle of fences and sheds, all the same colours of red, brown and grey. And off to one side the trains with cars piled with coal shunting past, clanging and grinding in front of the station.

I folded my hands and waited, waited for my mother to open the door, come in and put her arms around me. *It was just a mistake*, she would say. *Don't be silly. I would never leave you.* Then she would take my things from the dresser and put them in the suitcase, and we would slip away, just the two of us, without telling anyone we were going home. . . .

I sat there till my stomach started to growl, my eyes puffy and hot, my cheeks tight from crying. I heard rustling outside the door, then Arch's heavy boots on the stairs. After a minute I went and opened the door a crack. By the doorjamb was a bag of pink chicken bones.

I crunched and sucked on the splintery candy, the chocolate inside like a prize, a sweet consolation. I ate until my tears tasted like cinnamon. Then finally I crept downstairs, where Hettie pressed me to her apron and said, "It ain't so bad, now. You'll get used to it. She's only gone for a while."

*

At the time I had no idea "a while" could stretch into years, though perhaps Hettie knew it might. The first days and weeks without my mother I half expected to be placed on the train and shunted away, in fact I waited for that to happen. It kept me from missing her the way I would have had I known I'd been left behind. But as the weeks wore on and nothing changed, I became grateful for Hettie's inaction, even Arch's grumpy silence, as if all of us were just waiting to see what happened. Maybe Hettie saw things she liked in me, the way I made my own bed and dried dishes, and started thinking of me as a help, not just a child. She started sending me to the bakery across the tracks for bread, pressing the coins into my hand, and doling out chewing gum whenever Arch was in the coalshed or underneath the Ford. Perhaps her life *was* getting better; I still remember the morning Sears brought the automatic washer, and Arch moved the old washboard and wringer out to the barn.

I was too little then to wonder where she got the money after so many years of doing things the hard way, though maybe I sensed it came from my mother. As summer wore on we heard from her less and less; at first she had called every Sunday night to say things were fine. She was extra-busy now, she said, cleaning summer homes for her "clients", getting chauffeured down the coast to work. She promised to come get me by fall.

A week or so before school was to start, around the end of August, Hettie got Arch to take us down to the end of Atlantic Street, past the tar pond and the old coke ovens, and asked him to let us off by the cliff. He waited in the car while we waded through the bushes with our enamel bowls, picking our way around the shallow coalpits. The ocean was that dark blue, the sun at that far-off tilt that means summer's over, and I was feeling anxious. Hettie knelt down, half-filling her bowl with blueberries and huckleberries, while I mostly picked to eat, trying to think about pie rather than new shoes and scribblers, the black shadow of where I would be in September.

"Good teachers up the Grey school, I hear," Hettie said, sifting leaves out of her berries. "I think we'll send ya there. That's where yer mother went." Then Arch started tooting for us to hurry up, the question of where I'd go decided just like that.

I went into grade five as if I'd lived in Blackett all my life.

At recess one day the teacher asked who my mother was, and when I told her she smiled and said, "Oh yes, I remember, she married a MacNeil." It wasn't too long before the girls let me join in skipping—one of them, Wanda Bonnar, said her mother knew my mother when *they* were at school.

Every day Hettie would get after me to invite someone home to play. But I never did, no, I had enough of them at school, the other girls with their braids and bright pink skipping ropes.

"Girl yer age needs friends," Hettie would say, bustling around getting supper while I sat at the table doing sums. I wasn't unhappy—I was glad to let schoolwork keep me busy, and to get away from those excited voices when the bell rang. Even when my mother's calls stopped coming as often.

But then my birthday came, and I began to worry: what kind of cake, if any, would Hettie bake for me? What would my mother send? The cake, as it turned out, had only one candle, though I was turning nine—the stub of a hurricane candle stuck in the middle of a square cake, white with pink icing. Arch had found the candle in the coalshed at the last minute, because Hettie's knees were bad that day and she couldn't go uptown for real candles. After supper she disappeared into the pantry, the dishes still on the table, and limped out with the cake, singing "Happy Birthday" in a wavery voice. Then she handed me a china cup and saucer, so thin it was almost translucent, painted pink with chipped gold daisies and lettered, *For a Good Girl.*

"My mother gave it to me when *I* was nine," she said. "I guess I was saving it for you." I was disappointed it wasn't a toy, something bright and sturdy, something to play with. But more than that I was upset that my mother had forgotten to call.

She did phone a few months after that, one night in early spring. I could hear Hettie downstairs speaking with her. "Lord, no, she's been in bed for hours," I heard my grandmother explaining, waiting for her to hang up and come upstairs to talk to me. She didn't, choosing instead to tell me at breakfast.

"Yer mother's comin' to visit," she said.

"To *visit?*"

"She didn't say for how long. Close your mouth while you're eating."

"Will I be going back with her?" My cornflakes had gone mushy, the metallic taste of milk was on my tongue.

"Git a move on or you'll be late." That was all she said till later, when I came home after school. Hettie was outside bringing in the wash, it being a Monday.

"She's here," she muttered, her lips pinched around a clothespeg. "Well, go on in—I don't know how long she's plannin' to stay." She snapped the sheets in the wind, tucking the corners under her chin to fold them.

My mother was sitting at the table, stirring milk into some tea, her gloves still on. She started when she saw me.

"I was going to come up and meet you," she said, half rising and grabbing for my hand as I came towards her. I let her pull me to her, the slippery fabric of her blouse against my face, her hand smoothing the top of my head.

"My Jesus, you've grown up so."

I was glad when Hettie came in and I didn't have to answer.

The visit lasted exactly five days. Most of the time I was at school, the rest of it was business as usual. Homework, then supper and dishes, a few games of Chinese checkers with Hettie and Arch later if there was time. Hettie was always around, it seemed, so there was no chance for my mother to talk to me. Once or twice she joined in our games, but she never looked as though she was enjoying it much. Hettie would have to nudge her when it was her turn to move. One night when I was brushing my teeth I heard Hettie say that she was doing me no favours being half there, half someplace else. And when my mother left I have to say I felt relieved, the way I did when I finished a page of math. After that she came to see me a few more times, usually just before people's spring cleaning, till finally Hettie told her the visits upset my schoolwork, that maybe she should wait for summer, when she could see more of me. It was Arch of all people who passed on this bit of information; I figured then that it must be true, and that Hettie was right.

It wasn't until a couple of months ago—just after I turned eighteen, when Hettie was dying in hospital—that I really started to think about the teacup, to realize what she had given me. I had moved from the attic down to her tidy double bed, the small pink room with its white curtains fluttering in the draft, the noise of trains beyond. It was a room I'd hardly dared enter before, Hettie's little sanctuary you knew better than to go into. When Arch took her to the hospital I guess I wanted to be as close to her as I could, in my own way. I brought the cup down from the attic and put it on her dresser. The night Hettie died I was in her bed reading—a paperback romance, I think it was—and the next morning Arch tapped on the door to tell me she was gone. That's when I stopped wondering why Hettie never gave my mother the cup, and saw why she had given it to me instead.

The morning of the funeral we woke to a silver thaw. My mother arrived in a small blue car—*a friend* had driven her up from Halifax, she said, stepping into the kitchen. I knew her right away, though she was shorter and younger-looking than I expected. She didn't bother taking off her coat.

"Buddy come in for a cuppa tea?" Arch asked, loosening his tie. We still had a couple of hours before the service.

"He'll wait," she said, her eyes all over me. Through the fogged-up window I could see the man out in his car, smoking and blowing on his hands to warm them.

"*Nancy,*" she said, and I could see she was going to cry.

"You come all this way and you *missed* her," I said, pushing past her and Arch standing there with the teabags in his hands. Her coat smelled of the cold, her breath like cigarettes and coffee.

"I'm sorry," she said, holding out her hands.

"Tough, ain't it?" I cried, reeling away from her, making for the porch. Then I grabbed my coat and ran outside, sliding across the glazed yard. *Hettie, Hettie, Hettie,* I sobbed, skidding through the gate and over the icy tracks. Everything was still, in a silvery glare; trees bent and glittering with ice, snow reflecting the sky, a clear cold blue. Not a cloud to be seen, but the sun too weak to do any good.

Epitaph

Roger waited in the car while I went in, I asked him to. It didn't seem fair, somehow, dragging a stranger into the middle of everything. We'd spent the night at a motel in Sydney; he'd been good enough to drop everything the minute Arch called, and drive me up. A busy man, Roger, a travelling tire salesman. "What the hell," he'd said, "I *like* driving. Don't worry about it." After the news about Ma, I was in no shape to argue.

Arch had sounded ticked off, maybe even a little hurt, when I phoned from the Tartan to say I wouldn't be over till next morning. "Why don'tcha stay here?" he wanted to know.

"Look, you got enough on your hands, with the funeral and all." What I meant was I needed time—a couple of rum and Cokes, then a decent night's sleep—before going there and facing Arch and Nancy.

"I know *someone*'ll be glad to see ya," he said before he hung up. (I'm not sure what he meant by that; the older Arch gets, the harder he is to figure out.)

I could tell Ma was gone the minute I walked in. It was an awful shock, the emptiness like a cold hand. The stove on with nothing cooking, Ma's old brown coat in the porch, her plastic bonnet hanging from the pocket. Arch and Nancy were in the kitchen killing time, Nancy shockingly tall and skinny in a shiny-looking grey dress and too-high heels.

"Ma," I mumbled, looking at them, one to the other. Arch cleared his throat and reached for the King Cole tin over the stove. Nancy had put the kettle on, they had the can of milk right out on the table, no pitcher.

I couldn't take my eyes off her—she was taller than me, I swear, her eyes dark and smudged from crying.

"Nancy?" I held my hands out to her, no sound but kindling snapping, the clinkers settling in the fire. "Jesus, I hardly recognize you."

She teetered past me, her face like chalk under her splotchy makeup. Full of hate, slamming outside in her flimsy shoes. For a second I almost followed—till I thought, sweet Jesus, who could blame her? At least Roger wasn't in the house to see it; God knows what he thought when she came flying out.

"Easy on 'er," said my brother, setting the teapot on to simmer. "Sure yer friend won't come in? Jesus cold out there, ya know." His face was pink, freshly shaved but for some stubble he'd missed near his ear. He smelled of aftershave; his white shirt was still creased from the package.

Ma, I thought again, stirring the thick milk around and around in my cup. The sweet curdled smell made me cringe. "It's as if she's just gone up to the co-op for something, be back any minute. . . ."

"Jesus." Arch looked away and shook his head. "Like the goddamn Second Coming. You'd know about that now, wouldn'tcha? Away so long and suddenly poppin' in."

"I wish ya'd phoned me sooner. I didn't know she was that bad."

"Awww," he said, wiping up the ring from his cup, tossing the dishrag into the sink. "It wouldn'ta made no difference."

Outside I heard Roger start the car, the engine revving in the cold air.

"Hell of a time to go," Arch tried joking then. "Goddamn middle of winter. Just like her, too."

I tried to laugh, staring at my hands in my lap, the lines like the stitching on a softball. When I looked up again he was crying.

At the funeral Nancy wouldn't look at us. She sat several

pews back with some friends, two girls dressed the same way, their bangs teased up into a crest. You could hear them sniffling, purses being zipped open for Kleenexes. I couldn't stop staring at the smooth beige casket, couldn't stand thinking of *her* inside.

"You never got to see 'er," Arch reminded me, gripping my elbow on the way out. Nancy was ahead of us, huddled between her friends, their hair swirling up in the wind.

"Can ya stay long enough to help me go through her stuff?" he wanted to know. I shrugged, feeling weightless as a bird under my thick black coat.

I helped Arch wash cups and make sandwiches, then set out on plates some of the baking people had brought, fancy squares with bright cherries, little marshmallows. I put away the pies and casseroles for Arch, for later. Neighbours and some of Ma's ladies from church came, staying long enough to gulp down some tea. When they left I followed my brother upstairs.

"Nancy's kinda taken 'er over," he laughed nervously as we entered Ma's room. The weak winter light seemed to blanch the dingy wallpaper, everything worn and faded, not at all like Ma's room the way she'd kept it. Her white slip hung over the back of a chair, one strap frayed and held together with a tiny gold safety pin.

It was like walking in on her, somehow. Like the time I'd stumbled in when she was in the tub, her thin breasts above the grey bathwater, or when as a child I'd catch her getting dressed, the straps cutting into her pale shoulders. How could I believe she wasn't there, her old jewellery box on top of the dresser, the tatted runner now furred with dust. Her wedding ring in a chipped blue dish. I'd never seen it off her hand.

When I slipped it on Arch coughed.

"I told Nancy she could have it."

After that we didn't talk, busying ourselves with sorting through the closet. Emptying drawers of tangled grey underclothes, bundles of papers bound with cracked rubber bands. Letters, report cards—Nancy's. There were a couple of photographs, one of Ma with the oldest boys lined up outside the back door, Ma's face stern and smooth, her glossy dark hair pulled up in a bun. Another of Arch and me at the beach eating oranges, freckle-faced and squinting for the camera, Ma out of the picture but for a dark sliver of arm.

I shut my eyes and tried to remember that day: the smell of the oranges and the sand, the sting of orange peel under my nails. Ma warm and smiling beside me, but vague and faceless. Her wide-brimmed straw hat, her good print dress—got up as if for church, not a picnic. Her laughter, her cautious shouts not to go out past our knees. I could remember all of these details, but not *her*, not how she was *apart* from me.

"Remember that day?" I nudged Arch.

"No," he said, piling things into a green garbage bag. "No, can't say that I do." He started digging through a pile of sewing, plastic bags full of unravelled knitting, half-pieced quilt scraps.

"What's this?" he said, dragging out a small brown trunk from under the pile.

"Jesus if I know," I tried to joke, sorting through some faded dresses, laying them on the bed. "Don't remember that at all." I stopped what I was doing to watch Arch open it.

Digging through the ragged tissue paper, he brought out hats. One, a stiff black velvet with ripped netting, I recognized right away: the hat she'd worn to my father's funeral. But the other—? A soft brown velvet, with a cream-coloured rose, frayed in spots, musty but still elegant. I picked it up and put it on. But it was too small, wouldn't go on without crushing my hair.

"Lordy," Arch started laughing. "Now where the hell would she uv worn that, I wonder." Then he softened. "Look, you see anything ya want, just take it. I got no use for the stuff, and Nancy says she got everything she wants. Go on, take them hats—they're no good to me."

"It's all right," I said, replacing them, covering them with tissue. Arch clicked his teeth and shut the lid, shoving the trunk back in the closet. "But I will take the letters, the ones I wrote her."

*

That night at the motel, I tried calling Nancy while Roger was out getting cigarettes. Arch said she was still over at her friend's, he didn't know when to expect her.

"Try 'er again in the morning," he said, and I explained that we'd be leaving first thing, my friend had work to attend to back in Halifax.

Later, while Roger sat propped up in bed drinking a beer and watching Home Box Office, I lay there thinking of Ma, a crazy mishmash of things. That day at the beach when we were kids, the way she used to play the organ sometimes if Pa was at work, then never after he got sick. A couple of times I almost phoned Arch back, not to ask for Nancy but to see what he *did* remember, if not the beach. How, for instance, we used to sit on the front steps after supper if Pa was working late, and listen to her playing, the notes wheezing from the upstairs window. How other kids would sometimes drift over, crowding around the bottom step till it started getting dark. And how Ma would come to the door and call us, her voice high and shrill in the soft damp air.

The next morning after breakfast I dialled Arch's place once more. It took my brother forever to pick up the phone.

"Nancy's still sleepin', I think. She never come in till real late last night," Arch said, as surly as if he'd just woken himself.

I told him Roger was anxious to hit the road, said I'd wait while he went and got her up.

"Why don'tcha stop in here on yer way? Give Nancy time to git herself organized," Arch muttered, before going off to yell up the stairs.

"Yer wanted on the phone, girl," I could hear him saying. He sounded almost as he used to when we were teenagers, when he'd answer the phone and it would be some fella looking for me. Both of us taking care not to twig Ma's interest.

When Nancy finally came on she sounded tired, as if grief and anger had all but worn her out.

"What is it you want anyway?" she said, sighing.

I paused, groping for the right thing to say.

"Look," I began, "now that Ma's gone, I s'pose you and Arch—"

"Uncle Arch and I will do fine."

I swallowed, took a deep breath.

"What I mean is, you could always come down to Halifax. For a while. Till you figure out—"

I could almost see her clenching her teeth, ready to spring back from me the way she had before the funeral.

"Figure out what?" She coughed.

"Well. While you look for a job or whatever, now you're just about finished school." Then it hit me. "You're not gonna stay *here*, are you?"

It was as though I could hear her mind working.

"I don't know," she said at last, in a voice so soft I could imagine her weeping now. "I don't know what I'm going to do."

And with that galling cageyness of hers, she added: "But I'm staying with Arch till I decide."

Acknowledgements

I wish to thank Pamela Donoghue, Sheree Fitch, my uncles and aunts, especially Elizabeth, and my husband Bruce Erskine and our sons, Andrew, Seamus and Angus, for their patience. I'm also deeply grateful to the Explorations Program of the Canada Council, for its generous financial assistance, and to Kate Currie of the Beaton Institute, University College of Cape Breton. Thanks, finally, to my editor Gena K. Gorrell, for her invaluable expertise.